I0672701

A Pleasure Jaunt
With One of the Sex Workers
Who Don't Exist
in the
People's Republic of China

Tom Bradley

NeoPoiesis Press, LLC

NeoPoiesis Press
P.O. Box 38037
Houston, TX 77238-8037

www.neopoiesispress.com

A Pleasure Jaunt with One of the Sex Workers Who Don't Exist in the
People's Republic of China by Tom Bradley
ISBN 978-0-9832747-8-0 (paperback : alk. paper)
        1. Fiction: Short Stories. I. Bradley, Tom

Printed in the United States of America.

First Edition

Contents

Injuring Eternity

As if you could kill time without injuring eternity.
Thoreau, *Walden*

Every morning I killed all the sinners on earth.
—Psalm 101. 8

One early morning in the latter half of my elementary school career, the local Mormon TV station made a mistake and actually broadcast something stimulating. It was a silent short subject, one of those ancient slapstick orgies, the first I'd ever seen. The proper frame-rate to run such movies hadn't yet been recollected from the misty past. Everyone thought they were supposed to be fast-motion and jerky. That false quality caught my eye, and I asked my dad what in the hell I was looking at.

"Watch the language," he said. (For a second, I thought he was referring to the titles.) "It's an example of primitive movie making."

Dad's antepenultimate was one of my buzzwords. The other was *heuristic*. I was in a serious do-it-yourself phase. It was the pre-rental video era, yet I had managed to see *The Swiss Family Robinson* seven times. That's how many different grownups I'd pestered into driving me all the way downtown. (This was also the pre-suburban mall era.)

"Like how primitive? Could I make a movie like that by myself?"

"Well..."

"I mean with just stuff in the backyard."

Dad was holstering his slide rule and heading toward the door on his way to support the family. But he paused a couple dutiful seconds and rubbed his freshly scraped chin. "Backyard stuff, eh?" he said. "Are you including the old Bridgestone tires and the jugs of lawn chemicals? And that broken Frigidaire the neighbor kids like to play house in? Or just *Swiss Family Robinson*-type stuff?"

He knew where I was headed.

I had read Defoe's contribution to this genre of prepubescent male fantasy, probably the kiddy version, as well as *Lord of the Flies*. At such an early point in our father/son heart-to-heart, I wasn't thinking of much more than twigs and tendrils in various combinations. In that halcyon period before the eighth grade and excessive LSD, educators tended to tell me I was "borderline-precocious." But I needed a nudge from novels and movies into the anchored empiricism of physical substances and processes. I would oblige Dad to give me my nudge, even if it doomed him to miss his usual jump on the morning rush hour.

"Interesting question," he said, and sat down, his briefcase poised on his knees for a speedy exit. And he murmured it once again, more vaguely. "Interesting question." (Was he trying to convince himself?) "Hollywood on a shoestring. Minus the plastic ferrule."

He winked at me. But I didn't know what a ferrule was, so I didn't wink back or chuckle or anything like that. I probably should have.

"Well," he said, sitting up a tad straighter, "we moderns have a considerable technological history behind us. To be fair, you'd have to give yourself a sort of racial amnesia, and start with no prior knowledge of the properties of materials. Or that they even had 'properties.' You'd need to do an awful lot of research very quickly. In your shoes, my boy, I would fail immediately." Without quite standing up, he reached out his extraordinarily long arm and groped for the knob on the door.

I wonder, in hindsight, as they say, if such a ready admission of fallibility on the part of my lifetime default role model shocked little Tommy, me. I don't recall any emotional reaction to that paternal caving-in, except maybe impatience.

I detained the old man and somehow, with my boy-level locutions, got this general idea across to him: the way I saw it, there was no obligation to "be fair" and "start with no prior knowledge of the properties of materials." I could remain the modern youngster that I was, with a more-or-less clever pre-teen layman's knowledge of technological history—but with an admittedly peculiar need to make art from absolute scratch.

"Obviously," I piped (or words roughly to this effect), "poetry and painting and song and dance are simple to arrange. A movie is more of a challenge."

"'Challenge' is putting it mildly."

"And I'm giving myself the maximum believable luck."

"Which you'll need. Especially with regard to the animals, vegetables and so forth that we could scrape—or, rather, *you* could scrape—?"

Dad looked at me in an odd sort of way. Was he offering to pitch in, or trying to be gentle about begging off? He and I always did have a rough time communicating our basic desires and motivations to one another.

"—that *one* could scrape from the trees or dig from the dirt."

Maybe he was just hoping to scare me off in time to get to his classroom before his beloved disciples wandered off. It was impossible to tell. I followed my father's glance as he averted it from my face to the tube.

It was turning out to be a downright Mack Sennet festival. Some Latter-Day-Saint at the TV station must have had a nervous breakdown and become non compos mentis. Here it was, kiddy-narcotizing hour, yet "Augie Doggy and Doggy Daddy" were nowhere to be seen. I could swear, in retrospect, that they were even forgetting to insert the breakfast confection commercials. But that's impossible.

In apparent dismay, Dad watched five or six rickety Model-T's barreling down a Los Angeles back street. They wove in and out among themselves in fast motion, like a squad of basketball players on drill.

His voice took on a slightly pleading tone when he said, "How about if you just did the screenplay? Your big brother and I

3

laid some nice flat flagstones around the sort-of patio, and I could show you how to make a nice Cub Scout fire for charcoal, and you could scribble—I mean, write—"

He knew it was no go. I may have received a calling for it, but no red-blooded American boy wants to be seen, out of doors, frittering away his vitality on the wimpy alphabet, to go around with people snickering cruelly behind his back, "There goes a print man," and applying to him that most contemptuous of modifiers: *bookish*. Far better to be called a Nancy-boy. Whatever reading and writing I did was a death secret outside the house.

Without acknowledging his suggestion, I told him what I wanted. For example, tearing branches off the trees and ornamental pyracantha bushes for fuel, melting the contents of the sandbox to manufacture camera lenses—

"—and, also, I guess, I'll need to siphon off some glass to make insulation for my generator and electrical components, since rubber trees will not be available, and I've declared the old tires off-limits—"

I was trying to stick to Thoreau's ideal, yet couldn't picture the operation without electricity. A generator seemed requisite.

But Dad said, "Whoa back, Trigger." (He thought I was still on Roy Rogers.) "I can tell you right off the bat, kid, that home-made electricity will not be plausible."

Thus, with that single flat and unqualified pronouncement, my dream was shattered to shivers, like substandard glass. Throttled at birth. I couldn't believe such summary betrayal was possible within the nuclear family. What was this, Attic tragedy?

Just from the way he enunciated the words *home-made electricity*, Dad made my whole idea sound so unworthy of consideration. Building a generator involved too much. Everyone should know that, should have it pre-wired in his brain at birth, if not braided in his DNA at the moment of conception, for Christ's sake, as a basic rudiment of the common sense God gave a newt. My ambition of from-the-ground-up electronics was so infantile and preposterous, evidently, that I decided not to bother to ask him why.

But, I asked my sullen self, what was so insuperable? Dig up a little iron for the magnets, some copper for the coils, insulate where necessary with home-made glass—I wasn't planning on mega-watts here. I assumed that the old man was just getting, shall we say, *mature* and unambitious. Or, even more unforgivable, he was withholding permission for fear of my electrocuting myself. I elected to pout like a teenager in a movie.

That pout brought forth a weary sigh. "How sharper than a serpent's tooth," he groaned in body language. He took his briefcase off his knees, set it down on the linoleum, and plugged the distant percolator in, barely unbending his phenomenal arm.

"Do you really think," he said, "that you, or we, or anybody, confined to the backyard, without the aid of shovels and picks—"

I decided that Dad was being defeatist. Or else he was just coming on like the typical absent American father, unconcerned with his own spawn's intellectual development. This guy was not heuristic.

"—and, even if you dug deep enough, straight down to bedrock, and somehow hacked through that, using your fingernails presumably, and scritched and scratched and nibbled and bothered your way clear down to the Mohorovicic Discontinuity, do you honestly reckon, son, that you could come up with the ingredients for this generator? And collect enough of the various metals for your electronics? I don't mind telling you that it's highly unlikely—"

My face fell. I was not quite past that stage of development where tantrums are effective. Large as I was for my age, I could throw some elemental doozies. The whole block lived in dread of my hissy fits.

"Careerist," I hissed under my breath as Dad stole a furtive glance at his watch.

"—but not altogether impossible," he hastened to add, in a higher pitched voice, yanking his cuff down over the crystal. "I mean, if we're talking theoretically now."

"Theoretical is good," I said, in a soft but intense voice. I looked ominously down at my feet.

"After all," said Dad, sounding like a slightly depressed shoe salesman, "our backyard is situated within coughing distance of the world's largest open-pit copper mine, right?"

"And all I want is a little buzz," I moaned.

"And you're probably right about glass insulation—"

He gave me a "there's my bright boy" cuff on the side of the head, as a sort of consolation prize, mussing my imitation Beatle haircut with patronizing affection.

"But," said Dad (and he accompanied himself with stealthy motions of the shoulders, trying to ease the following notion into my little brain without chafing against any raw edges), "the result will be such a big cumbersome thing, won't it? Such an inefficient generator will need a giant crank, don't you think? No, a treadmill. Some animate creatures will be required to provide traction. I don't see any oxen grazing out there." He waved his arms in what he obviously hoped would be a gesture of broad preposterousness. "What would you do? Enslave a few dozen of the neighborhood children?"

Now, I am sure that his conscious reason, at any rate, for saying the above was to discourage me further. As the official report card signer, he knew I was bringing home C-pluses and even an occasional B-minus in civics class. This was one American lad tolerably well indoctrinated in human equality and human dignity and human freedom and that shit. But Dad's voice had placed altogether too much emphasis on the key word not to introduce at least a few complications.

"That's fine," I said. "I can enslave."

I was still just normal enough, in those pre-Purple Haze and Orange Sunshine days, to have friends. They visited our backyard frequently enough to be considered natural constituents thereof, and thus comprised an exploitable resource, if one were willing to stretch a point. So, Father's helpful suggestion posed no special difficulty at all. It was but an afterthought, especially compared to the technical questions we had yet to grapple with. Not to mention the cosmological puzzles that would soon envelop the Bradley household.

Nor would press-ganging enough warm bodies to rotate the treadmill pose any particular physical challenge for the likes of young Tommy. I was busily expanding to my present six feet, nine inches, three hundred and twenty pounds. (Can't help it: basketball family, you know. My father holds a plausible claim to having invented the hook shot when he was a pro in a cage in Chicago, way back in the olden days; my second-cousin Bill Bradley played for the Toledo Twats or whoever, and then went on to become one of the next presidents of our nation; and my Mormon nephew Shawn Bradley is currently the NBA's premier shot blocker or something. I have no idea what team he plays for, but he's seven-foot-six, so he gets to be in Bugs Bunny movies. It's not fair).

I chose to be no less systematic with the problem of human bondage than with my more scientific quandaries. An economy was being built here, as well as a motion picture studio. Introducing slaves into that economy required, of course, a source of calories for those slaves to burn. I informed my dad (his face blanching the while—he was a Kennedy Democrat and a card-carrying member of the American Civil Liberties Union, Utah chapter) that I would feed my livestock on the crab apples that casually fell on our side of the redwood fence from the laden boughs of the neighbors' tree, which esculents we Bradleys rightfully owned, according to something like Anglo Saxon common law, probably.

This was getting serious for Dad. I could tell by the various colors his face was turning. Babies in bondage in the backyard, Simon Legree for an heir: it was time to wax seriously dissuasive. "Turn back, oh man, forswear thy foolish ways" is what they sang in the non-Mormon church we were supposed to be members of but never went near. But he knew better than to appeal to my higher nature and impulses. Any alert parent who understands the sheer contrariness of little boys' minds will choose indirection in a situation like this.

"Tommy, hang on. I mean, it's very good that you've provided for your, er, employees' dietary needs. But why don't we back up a tad, shall we? Just for a moment. Don't you think a fellow might run out of fuel pretty quick making all these fires, lots of huffing and puffing, to prepare the copper? And especially the iron? There's only two trees out there."

Two and a half, actually. They were black locusts, and they filled the whole block with seminiferous things every year that caused the Mormons to resent us. Popularly known as a "trash tree," the black locust is a loosely organized being, the farthest thing from hardwood, and couldn't be a more inefficient source of fuel for very hot fires. Dad was right. The sorry organisms would be cakes of dead carbon in no time. If I was a scribbling poofter we might have something to talk about here. But I most emphatically was not.

So even something as simplistic as a blast furnace was proving no less impermissible than the generator itself. My dreams and ambitions of artistic self-expression, still sparkling with the moisture of youth, were popping like spit bubbles. I said nothing. Instead I just let my little face fall, once more, to tummy-button level, with that disappointment, that disenchantment, so chilling to a parent of future teens.

"This is not heuristic," I whispered.

Father yet again backed off from his dismissal. He was turning out to be one of those modern American parents who have difficulty saying no and sticking with it. Instead he tried gently to persuade his impulsive boy from such a dead-end path.

"You may tear down and set fire to the redwood fence—"

"Thanks, Dad."

"—if it's not too adulterative for your program."

"What's that supposed to mean? Thou shalt not—?"

"No, no. Outside stuff, you see. Not occurring naturally within your topographical perimeter. Violates your own ground rules. That fence has been creosoted and varnished and painted god knows how many times, with the devil only knows how many different store-bought compounds. For Hell's sake, creosote comes from the destructive distillation of coal. And do you think, if coal was anywhere near our backyard, Brigham Young wouldn't have caused this whole neck of the woods to be gutted long ago?"

He paused and looked at me with a peculiar sort of intensity. I couldn't tell if his question was rhetorical.

"Um," I said, "well—"

"But, let's say you loosen up a tad on your no-outside-stuff requirement (your big brother would say 'cop out'), and go ahead and consume the fence. Even still, depending on how many sequels and prequels the entertainment market will bear, you may wind up needing to grow more trees. And you know what that takes."

"Time?"

"You said it." With the finality of a coffin maker driving home his ultimate fastener, he intoned, "Time, my boy, is one commodity that can't be stretched out, or fudged on, or substituted for, or snuck past. Time's unlike creosote. You can't cop out on that."

"Time's unlike creosote? Can I quote you?"

"You have only so much. And I have almost none."

Dad looked at the clock. Pavlovian class bells would be ringing now at his place of employment. He visibly fought the conditioned reflex to reach into his briefcase and fetch his roll book.

"Time is no problem," I said—and learned that fact only as I uttered it. I didn't know why it was true, nor why I'd been assuming it so deeply that I hadn't bothered to verbalize that requirement (or lack thereof) before now. It gave us both pause, this odd little utterance of mine.

My father heard it well enough, and nodded in agreement, with a similar lack of consideration. We didn't even glance at the television.

I said it again: "Time's no problem."

Not forgetting to feign another sigh of resignation, Dad looked at me with unmaskable pleasure in his eyes. He took pains to restate my notion, his boy's new insight, so that it would sound as nearly rational as possible—for now. This was still supposed to be merely a scientific discussion.

"Of course," he said slowly, "time's no consideration. I mean, not for someone your age, right?"

"Right, Dad. Us kids have no sense of—"

"Time. Right."

His roll book, for the moment at least, was forgotten.

"Especially," I added, "since, unlike you, Dad, I've got nowhere in particular to go today." I beamed a proud grin at him, which his own face reflected like a convex mirror.

I was undergoing my most recent suspension from school, a regular thing for me. I am fortunate to have undergone brathood in the days before Ritalin and Prozac and Luvox. Otherwise I would have been doped into submission instead of banished. Not a bad boy, exactly, I was just following parental orders when I refused to stop arguing the origin of species with a certain sacerdotal functionary who spent his weekdays posing as a public school teacher. (This guy, incidentally, was never one of the educators who told me I was "borderline precocious.")

It was this crew-cut crypto-proselytizer's "Utah history" class from which I was continually being ejected, because my fourth- or fifth-generation excommunicated Jack-Mormon atheist dad sent me there each morning with a bad attitude and a head full of amino acids, primordial soup and other evolutionary decoctions, and a directive to challenge the "Elder" on the doctrines of Creationism.

This was just one of the several ways in which Dad, in his own words, "systematically corrupted" me, his priceless boy. He had started the process early on, trying to subvert my socialization already in kindergarten, about the time Teller launched all that lethal Nevada sand in our faces. Filling my head with locally heretical doctrines would help ensure my never backsliding into some "hare-brained throwback Latter-Day-Saint crapola" as my nephew Shawn Bradley did. Bugs Bunny's co-star hawked the faith of Brigham Young in Australia for two years when he could have been earning about sixteen million bucks getting his nose and collarbones broken by ebony elbows in the NBA. The fans throw bottles at him and call him The Great White Ope because he looks and acts and sounds like an elongated version of Andy of Mayberry's fair-haired boy.

Rather than allow anyone in our branch of the clan to be sucked into such a downward spiral, Father was bent on getting me officially and publicly expelled from the second most potent disseminator of Mormon "culture," the Utah public school system. He would cite my permanent record to embarrass me into relenting if I ever, by some freakish twist of circumstance or some gross overdose of mind-bending drugs, decided to get baptized by full-immersion, and convert, like my seven-foot-six clown cousin, to the sect that had spilled and nearly expunged our very Bradley blood in one of the many episodes of savage tyranny that have since been deleted from the pages of early Utah State history.

So I cut my rhetorical teeth facing down the "Elder." He was a textbook paranoid-schizophrenic who had ninety-eight percent of the *Book of Mormon* memorized, and who, in order to be able to keep his own animalistic self-contained in his polygamist pants, simply had to believe that he bore no relation whatever to the naked chimps that hung their private parts between the bars at the zoo and flung excrement at people.

So far, my limited debating skills had only managed to get the lunatic to kick me out for brief periods. But I intended to be an obedient child, and to continue rubbing the rock salt of natural selection into the open sore that was the "Elder's" psyche, until I got an outright parole from formal education (every real boy's dream).

When and if I ever succeeded, I wasn't sure if Dad was planning on coughing up the exorbitant tuition for Episcopalian parochial school, or on home-educating me, as our polygamist friend Mr.Singer did with his own children before the state authorities came and shot him to death on his front porch for such lawless presumption.

Speaking of which, the ancient comedy flickering in front of us now jerked in a very big way, right off the reel. It stopped altogether, browned, and started to bubble, as it got stuck in whatever hot contrivance TV stations utilize to put film on the air. Someone at the station downtown, presumably the mad Mormon who'd started this sepia jamboree in the first place, acted fast, gave the thing a good thump, and got it going again, after only five or six seconds of the televisual equivalent of dead air.

"Still and all," said Dad, shaking his head slightly, like someone who's just been nudged awake in an auditorium, "um, as you said, time's no problem... yet, be that as it may... yes, even with the, er, scheduling restraints loosened up a tad..." He cleared his throat. "Even taking your, let's say, boyishly inchoate sense of time into consideration, there's still one bugaboo, one utter perplexity."

"A bugaboo?"

11

"The sheer size of the *energy* requirement here. You could place the entire student body of your elementary school under the yoke, for Christ's sake. Stake out a space as big as the whole block for them to twirl your treadmill—and that last bit's by far the most implausible: Brigham Young wouldn't allow your great-great-great-grandparents enough dry dirt to die on, in blatant violation of the Federal Homestead Act of 1862—"

He was back on track, and pouring coffee, oddly, into two cups.

"—but I still doubt you'd be able to get the amounts of energy, of *light*, you'd need for a movie. Tommy, I will have to go with my previous statement that no dynamo would be practicable—"

Again, my face fell. I was starting to feel stretchy around the hairline. But, before I could throw myself on the floor and start howling, he quickly said, "—or *necessary*."

But I didn't hear that promising qualification, because I was holding back tears (or maybe pretending to), and very obviously grasping for means to salvage not only the project, but my budding sense of self-esteem. I hiccoughed, bravely, "Well, gee-whiz, Dad. What about a wet cell?"

The "Elder" had shown us how to build one in pseudo-science class the previous year. (Such tinkering was devoid of overt cosmological implications and hence permissible.) I knew the salt requirement for a wet cell could be easily met. All I had to do was glance out the window at the blighted landscape of my birthplace. Neighbors of Scandinavian and Anglo-Saxon descent, but with the faces and hands of Essenes, squeaked past in brand new cars, undercarriages already rotted away. Salt was no problem. I could maintain an ample supply just knocking deposits off the rain gutters after the briefest of April showers.

"Well," my father replied, with monumental amounts of patience in his voice, "let's talk about that, okay?" He felt obliged, like the competent nurturer he was, to tell me what was good about my fancies before giving them the thorough trashing they deserved.

"It's true—and I am so proud of you for learning this at school, Tommy—that a saline solution is needed for a wet cell.

Injuring Eternity

But it would have to be even bigger than the generator. It would have to be a continental wet cell. Did I hear you wrong, or did you not say *just the backyard*? I thought this backyard thing was a spatial restriction, too. Was I wrong? Are you going to spread the contents of our god-damn garden clear across the—"

He was getting a bit frustrated and starting to treat me like another grownup. That was no good. So I said, "Teacher says the Great Salt Lake is a wet cell battery. That's not continent-sized. They bisected it into halves of unequal salinity with the causeway, and—"

"And it generates about one thirty-thousandth of a volt every year." Father fanned his arm toward the window, at the dead sea on the horizon, which suppurated under its customary shroud of sulfur dioxide. "You're really going to get great picture quality with that. Talk about *film noir*. Your teacher has his head up his sea gull-worshipping ass."

Dad got serious now. It was time to light up a cigarette. Being the most emphatically non-Utahn of all mainstream tobacco products (designed and marketed, as they were, to appeal to African Americans, whom the Mormon scriptures describe as "black and loathsome"), Kools were what he smoked, in those days before experts decided all that extra menthol crystallized the lining of the lungs to no wholesome effect.

"Tommy," he huffed secondhandedly in my face. "Son. My boy. Think of a movie. Think of all of the brightness coming from a movie. That's a reflection of what the projector is sending to the screen. Today's screens are efficient reflectors. Your screen would be the backs of large pieces of bark or mold. How would you go about getting light to pass through the image with enough power so that you could actually see it? That would be about two intensities of a typical overhead projector. Just a whole damn bunch of light, Tommy. Bags and bags of light. Powered by proportional amounts of electricity. And it must follow, as the night the day, and all that crap, that your wet cell is an even dumber idea than—"

"We could use magnesium," I countered. "I bet there's some out there. Teacher says it's the eighth most abundant ele-

13

ment in the earth's crust. Or else I could derive it from the chlorophyll in the plants."

Even though he must've known, as a full-time professional educator, that sarcasm rarely works on the young, and certainly never twice in rapid succession, he couldn't curb the irony.

"Magnesium? That would be a very strange and short movie."

"Fuck it," I said. Little Tommy commenced skulking off to his bedroom to assemble model airplanes with that seductive-smelling glue.

Dad was on the verge of losing his son, a nation-wide malaise in that epoch. His tardiest beatnik grad-students would have been accumulating among the rows of desks about then, yet he felt constrained to reach out and buttonhole me. To all appearances, he started warming to the task. But that was deceptive, a desperate job of play-acting. He began talking fast, trying to haul his boy in and fasten him to his side with ropes of words. Dad had a counterproposal.

"No, no, no, no, no. Don't fuck it, son. Not just yet. Watch the language," he remembered to add. "Electricity is not necessary. I'm thinking solar. You know, Save the Trees. Your big brother and all the other cool college kids eat this stuff up. Sunshine, not that dark subterranean shit from Hell that you have to melt just to get it to behave. I'm thinking of the nice easy things ol' Sol helps to grow every day."

"Twigs?"

"Tendrils as well. Like that. Like our little plywood playhouse we built together in an earlier and less, um, complex period of your youth. Fond memory, right? Let's do that again. We'd build a small hut, like our playhouse, but with light seals all around, fashioned from tree sap and mud, and a small hole in a wall or two. If we could get a good beam of sunshine through this Latter-Day-Saint smog, that would project nicely. Oh, and we need bearings for the hut, because it's set on a rotational device so it can follow the sun, while the mice are turning the twig-and-tendril cage wheel to run the images through. This is going to look more like Jacquard's loom than Edison's Kinetoscope."

I decided that I liked the sound of that. The idea of a clickety-clack affair appealed to me. It was better than some hot sputtering thing, truer to my Flintstone roots, more like *The Swiss Family Robinson*. It had taken some doing, but this little representative of the newest generation of Bradleys was successfully weaned from directed drifts of electrons.

"A hut *cinematique!*" I hooted.

Father saw the habitual tension leave my face, and felt emboldened to say, "Now, son, by this time you will have manumitted the neighborhood kids from generator detail, as in free the slaves."

Hearing that, however, made me petulant again. I should have known there was a social program lurking behind this. "You never want me to have any fun," I whined.

"You know that's not true!" he cried, desperate to swap his social conscience and political convictions for some filial affection. But he failed to demur quickly or ardently enough to prevent my retiring, like Achilles, to sulk in my figurative tent.

I consulted the television in silence. It continued to serve an uninterrupted stream of pre-Depression slapstick, from a time when the majority of rank-and-file Hollywooders were bumpkins—like my extended family, come to think of it—and had thick-skulled notions of what was amusing, and what was permitted.

I only just consciously noticed something that my eyes had been registering for several minutes about these silent short subjects: most of the interest lay around the edges of the frame, where palm trees blew mournfully in an odd gray haze. It was an opportunity to see what southern Californian vacant lots looked like, back in the days when most (instead of today's mere many) members of the Bradley tribe were still living like the Flintstones, deep in the Utah mountains.

One of my buzzwords, as I said, was *primitive*, and I came by it honestly. It wasn't just *The Swiss Family Robinson* that piqued me. It was the Deracinated Family Bradley as well.

In the 1850's Mormon missionaries had enticed us all the way across the Atlantic from the coal mines of Sheffield, England (I don't know how we could have fit in the tunnels; maybe we worked behind the counter in the company store, fetching hardtack off high shelves), only to kick us almost immediately out of their territorially omnipotent church, and drive us naked into the wilderness. We howled at the moon and subsisted like Neanderthals and interbred for two generations, or maybe three (amid such genealogical chaos, spouses and spawn are difficult to differentiate), self-creating in a literal sense.

Unlike Mr. Thoreau, who was back east at the time having his camp-out, we did not hear "the rattle of railroad cars, now dying away and then reviving like the beat of a partridge." We heard grizzlies and timber wolves beating the hell out of each other just outside the glow of our campfire. And there were no trains within eight hundred miles.

It was only in the past sixty years or so that we Bradleys had begun to shamble back down from the federally designated Primitive Area, high and deep in the Rockies, where it's still legal to kill anything not worshipped by the aboriginals as long as you eat it. We'd stealthily settled among the very folks who had, for reasons still in dispute, chased us off like flatulent pets so long ago. Keeping a low profile, not receiving the benefit of the Mormon welfare system, the Bradleys were socially ostracized (thank Christ almighty: I'd have made a horrifying missionary). The only career opportunities open to the likes of us were sordid positions among the communists and alcoholics and other deviants at the non-Mormon university. If my boyhood's backyard was to be a self-contained unit, it would be modeled on my clan.

Only that summer we'd planted a great-grandma (or great-great-auntie—nobody knew) who, before senility claimed her, could sputter a few spasmodic syllables of the private language her cousins (siblings?) had invented among the stalagmites, Brontes without the basic literacy skills. Ours was one family that had not forgotten its victimological heritage.

Primitive was the buzzword, even like my father, still, in the most important parts of himself. He was a professor at that time, but remained a troglodyte under that thin tenure-track veneer. And it was starting to come out this morning, I could tell. Waylay the old man long enough, get him sufficiently bored and irritated with some insoluble problem, and the sagebrush lycanthrope would poke its damp snout through. Briefly bring out the Bradley, and then the instruction would start in earnest.

"Someone will have to be outside, rotating the hut *cinematique*, won't they?" asked Dad, not removing half-closed eyes from the screen. A little man with a big black hat and beard was being dunked headfirst in a rain barrel. "'Manumit *most* of the neighborhood kids' is what I should have said."

"Yeah," I grinned. "We'll need hut rotators."

"You can withhold freedom from two or three children," Dad sort of leered. "Selected for tractability more than strength, as this hut won't be all that difficult to move, if we get the bearings smooth and nice. I see a sort of pivoted roller system, using logs from the two and a half black locust trees. But they will need patience, these kiddy-chattels, to follow the sun, and steady little personalities. Real bourgeois types."

On television, raunchy mayhem was being perpetrated upon minor characters, recruited by the casting director and enticed with alcohol from Los Angeles skid rows. Their congenitally abnormal faces had been enhanced with pancake makeup and mascara to haunt you like details from a repressed childhood trauma. I couldn't have been more enchanted. We were looking at a division of our tribe who'd stumbled a little further west than the rest of us.

"I suggest," said Dad, "that little Latter-Day-Saint next door who wears glasses."

"LaMar Jacobsen?"

"And his plump sister. The one whose kitty-cat uses your sandbox as a latrine."

"Tiffany."

At the mention of that lugubrious name, Dad regressed even deeper into an atavistic back-tunnel accent. His upper canines began to chaw at his lower lip. "Named after the famous maker of *favrile* glass. Later we'll have a special use for her."

"How do you mean?"

He failed, or refused, to acknowledge my request for clarification.

"We build the hut for, say, seven people. Six customers and the exhibitor (you, I assume). I think we should also install a pedal device as a backup so that you, the exhibitor, can rotate the hut, just in case the wretches toiling outside die from sunstroke or malnutrition, or organize a strike, or burrow under the redwood fence while you're at the movies with your—um, where's the audience coming from?"

"Fishing for an invitation to the world premiere?"

"Not necessarily. But, if you plan on selling tickets, or, rather, bartering them off (as there'll be no currency that I've been informed of), shouldn't the population pool from which these patrons are drawn be a natural occurrence of the backyard?"

He was driving at something I was too young to cotton on to readily. I didn't pursue it, and neither did he, for the time being. As usual with such subjects, it was very tantalizing, but somehow better left alone.

He did appear to be genuinely warming to the task this time. As the pre-World War Two inhumanity escalated further on the television, Father was unable to avoid injecting himself a bit more assertively into the scheme: *"You'll* do all this?" he said with his eyes and arms. *"We'll* do it?"

He was ready to get this pesky pronoun question out on the table, finally. It was time to firm up the duty roster. He was prepared, maybe eager, to jump in. But he seemed willing to concede that this production might be qualitatively different from the playhouse we'd knocked together. It was little Tommy's individuality being produced from the ground here. Father himself was an already finished product, for better or worse, and now must act only in an advisory capacity, and as chief financial backer.

Also caterer. Since I wasn't planning to live like my human cattle on crab apples, I assumed I'd be coming indoors on a regular basis for a sandwich or so, maybe some macaroni and cheese, composed of ingredients bought with the salary earned on the job from which my demand for parental attention was keeping my father. Kindly, indulgent, he didn't trouble me with this obvious fact, which had so conveniently slipped my boyish mind. He would remain my victualler, steadfastly and without comment, for the eons required to grow my fuel trees and produce my equipment and make my masterpiece from scratch—because, as he always said, he was immortal.

Whenever the big question came up (and it often did, with a morbid tyke like me underfoot), he pleaded deathlessness. And it wasn't just the untarnished posthumous reputation guaranteed the inventor of a major advance in human culture, such as the hook shot. Dad was talking corporeal permanence.

Not a really deep thinker, my old dad: denying the basic fact of everything, the prime condition of organic existence, from whose pondering comes all serious and headlong action; ignoring when not explicitly contradicting this most obvious of all obviousnesses, up until his sixty-fifth or seventieth birthday, when his own experience finally started making it undeniable, even to himself. I got my cockamamie ideas about time's unimportance from him.

Just to check and see whether it was a generational thing, I've since asked several friends and acquaintances of my approximate age if their own fathers staked this mightily wrong-headed claim for themselves. Nobody said yes. It seems to have been a peculiarity all my dad's own, this notion of a personal earthbound incorruption. But still I suspect it was more offhanded than hubristic, more Far Western, somehow, than megalomaniacal.

So, the Bradley lad's nourishment was indefinitely provided for, and he had settled on an alternative energy source, and was actually quite content to allow the nearest yellow main-sequence star to project his movie. But, project it via what medium? It was no longer possible to put off dealing with a certain indestructible synthetic compound, as undying in fact as my father fantasized himself to be in person. This needed subtlety.

"All right, we're set," I said, enunciating with pursed precision the first-person plural for the first time today, deliberately roping Dad into it. (I knew that, with the sinister shit I was about to moot for consideration, adult supervision was recommended.) "We have just about everything we need," I chirped. "We have manpower and some fashionable, vitamin D-enriched sunshine. Oh, and, also, Dad, not to forget—we'd better get ourselves a supply of something transparent to put the pictures on, to shine the sun through. Right? Um, Dad? What's the name of that plasticky stuff real movie guys use for—"

But before I could go any further, or recollect the name, he jumped to his feet, spilling both cups of coffee, and blurted, "Do you know what the earliest photographs were made on?"

"Huh?"

"Plates of *glass*, Tommy!"

"Blades of—?"

"Plates. Of beautiful, clear, biodegradable glass."

He was being a bit too emphatic in contradistinguishing glass' relative purity and simplicity from the toxic convolutions of the material that had just been on the tip of my tongue. For unknown reasons Father suffered from a violent and unreasoning prejudice against the plasticky stuff. This animadversion evidently overrode his need to go to work and his responsibility to discourage me from time-wasting enterprises. I found myself wondering what sort of childhood trauma he could possibly have suffered in the ancestral cavern, involving the dreadful concoction.

"Yes, and," he panted, supportive parent that he remained even under duress, "we can use your smart sandbox idea. For this *glass*, you know? You'll have to comb out the shit of Tiffany Jacobsen's cat. Tidy little beast."

"'—comb the shit out of—'?"

"No, no. From the sand. Comb out. Remove the feline excrement. As in impurities."

"Clean the latrine. Gross."

"Nobody said science was fun. Unleash her brother from the hut bearings and have him do it—oh, damn."

"What? What?"

"Niter."

For a moment I was delighted. Was this a new secret dirty word from the universe of grownups? Perhaps an epithet? "Niter?" I said, eagerly.

"I suppose it's not impossible that our small backyard might yield niter to supplement the sand for primitive glass manufacture. Although I'm not sure of this at all. I guess," he said, vaguely looking toward the room where we threw most of the books, "we could look it up..."

"... Naw-w-w," we said in unison, after no undue pause. This was just a casual dad-son conversation between two amateurs with no particular scientific bent. Dad was a professor of economics. The slide rule was for figuring out goods and services, inputs and outputs, greed and need, human stuff, not the physical universe.

"Anyway," he said, "you'll have to round those slaves back up to dig for niter. Maybe, while they're at it, you could ask your youngsters to scratch up a little manganese, too, if it's not too much bother, like the Phoenicians did. They invented the process by accident. A ship laden with niter wrecked on their shore, and the gentle Mediterranean surf blended the spilled cargo with the sand, which later, at low tide, was subjected to heat when the sailors set their cauldrons on the beach for a cookout. Or something like that. I don't know if they always had cookouts after shipwrecks, but there you have it."

"Subjected to heat? I thought you said—"

"I changed my mind. We'll have to get your smelting operation back on line. Since you insist that we are blessed with the history of materials and ability to use them, we'll have to invent the blast furnace, just as you suggested earlier. My bright boy," he beamed, giving credit where credit was due, and mussing my fair hair again.

So, just like that, by arbitrary adult fiat, my dad declared my blast furnace permissible after all. Little Tommy, who had barely adjusted himself to less flammable techniques, complained that he was being taken on an emotional roller coaster ride.

"Speaking of rollers," said Dad, "you will recall that the bearings for the hut are logs, which leaves you that much less fuel. We'd probably only need one batch of glass if we did a good job. Nevertheless, son, I'm afraid that our beloved little playhouse, which we worked so hard together to build, will have to be razed. For the plywood."

"I don't want to be sickeningly sentimental or anything, Dad. But wouldn't it be easier to just whip up some of that plasticky stuff real movie guys use for—"

"Silver!"

"Huh?"

"We need some."

"But I thought this was a barter economy."

"Primitive photographs were silver halides prepared in the dark and exposed to light on glass plates. Do you have fillings in your teeth?"

"You know I do. You pay for them."

"I mean silver fillings. We need them for the halides. Do dentists still use silver these days? My head's packed with the stuff. How about yours? The sadistic pederast down the street charges like he's using platinum."

It was not mere oral hygiene being bandied about here. The removal of dentition in dreams, says you-know-who's much maligned book on the interpretation of same, always signifies patriarchal castration: the Father attempting (not consciously, but as an involuntary function of his very biology) to subsume and absorb, which is to say emasculate the son, according to basic psychoanalytic theory. I was not enthusiastic about this proposition. Unsure as to what alloys had been tamped into my own reamed-out molars, I crossed my little legs and said, "Hey, Dad! I know. How about if, while my slaves are digging for the niter and the magnesium—"

"Manganese."

"Whatever—"

"Not 'whatever.' You'd better get that one right."

"—what if the kids come upon a hoard of old silver Mormon pioneer-type coins, and we use them instead of my—"

A shudder, stemming not necessarily from either of my yet unshaven jaws, shook the last word off.

Desperate to avoid, or at least postpone, the ultimate Oedipal showdown, I was willing to stretch yet another point. I reckoned its having been buried in our backyard for more than a hundred years would somehow render this bullion permissible—unlike the old Bridgestone tires and the broken Frigidaire, which had only lain there rotting for about a decade. I was prepared to disregard any treasure trove statutes that might exist on the Utah law books.

"A hoard of Mormon specie?" scoffed my dad. "Untithed? Left unpillaged by Brigham Young, the greedy son of a bitch who nearly had us all killed over a couple acres of scrub oak?"

"But Gr'auntie said it was because we—"

And the phrase recurred: "Very unlikely, but not entirely impossible. Yes, I suppose you could get sufficient silver halides off this sad pittance left by the voracious cult. We're assuming a single-take operation, anyway. Due to paucity of fuel, we're only going to have one chance at our blast furnace. But, these few coins would be seriously defaced, I think, by the process. What about the archaeological interest?"

We both got a chuckle out of that. They weren't exactly owl drachmas.

"So," said Dad, appearing nearly tension-free for the first time all day (that shared chuckle must have been therapeutic), "if we were to be satisfied with a negative image movie run on glass plates, we could stop now, and I could go to work and get there just in time for lunch."

My little ears perked up, like a doggy's. Did this process end in a negative image? Why was I the last to know? That struck me as superb. It would look like death, which, as our morning confabulation progressed ever closer to lunchtime, asserted itself more and more as the theme of my production—though I wouldn't at that point have been able to say why. It does seem to me now that I was a little young to have death on the brain.

"Oh, boy! A negative image would be swell, Dad! Real avant-garde, and like that!"

"Remember," he said, confidently gathering up his briefcase, "we're looking at some really lousy picture quality here. You'll probably wind up with just vague gray shadows hulking around on the wall. Plato's cave-type stuff."

"I don't care."

I wasn't aiming for a sequel to *Cleopatra* with Burton and Taylor. Something more along the lines of very early *Little Rascals* before Farina grew testicles. Cinema naivete.

"And, it's all very, very unlikely—though not altogether impossible."

"That goes without saying."

"Good," said Father, "it's settled then." He lunged for the door on his first-string center legs. And here I thought we'd just been talking in principle.

I said, in a firm enough voice to arrest his progress, "One eensy-weensy question. About the silver—um, things."

"Halides. Silver halides."

"How do we get them to stick on the glass?"

"Oh, they're suspended—"

He caught himself up short, and shoved another Kool in his mouth to impede the flow of indiscretion. I'm sure my ears did another cocker spaniel twitch.

"Suspended from what? In what?"

"Nothing."

"Even I'm suspended *from* something. Today, at least. Or is it suspended *in* nothing? That doesn't sound heuristic. What the fuck are you talking about, old man?"

He was cornered. Once again the doorknob left his giant fist, and the chair received his buttocks. He sent his briefcase sailing across the room. Hook shot. The pleasant look left his old face, the enthusiasm seeped from his voice, and he murmured, just audibly, "Gelatin."

"Yeah? So? What's the big heart attack? Wait till the Mo-mos have a picnic, slide a twig through the fence slats, latch onto a plateful, suck out the tiny marshmallows, and it's show time."

"That's jello. What we need is gelatin, not just any old colloidal guck. It's animal jelly."

Dad paused, in the forlorn hope that such a notion would elicit an "Eeeew, for *ick*," and put his child off the cinema altogether. But it was no sissy-pants he was raising. Every regular boy loves mucus, in all its incarnations.

"Heuristic!" I crowed. "Earthworms are animals. We could use earthworms. It's easy to grow masses of earthworms if you know how. You would just stick your hand into the mass and withdraw it slowly, like when you're about to go fishing. Then you could harvest maybe enough animal snot for mixing with the tooth decay filling crap."

Dad spoke quietly. "You honestly don't care about picture quality. Do you?"

"Maybe I should go into TV."

"No! Gelatin is derived from the connective tissue of vertebrates. Not the secretions of annelids, you little—"

"Oh, I do beg your pardon if you please. And this nectar can be had by? From? How?"

"Not every man is blessed with a job he really enjoys," said Dad, his face filled with longing.

"Yeah, but don't you want your favorite son to do heuristics?"

"Hooves are the best source, pound for pound. I imagine most is cow now. Used to be horse. The glue factory. We'd have to skip just a whole bunch of work and sit around on our butts and wait for a herd of one or the other to stampede across the street and down our driveway. Or listen for large numbers of some sort of wild ungulate to clatter by and make inroads, migrations, establish habitual trails. Ethologists call them *desire paths,* I believe. A hole of appropriate size would have to be kicked in the redwood fence. I feel like doing that now."

"I thought we burned it down already."

"Figures. I doubt many hoofed creatures were wandering past before Big 'n Hung and his ninety-seven wives showed up with their ox carts. Just lizards and Utes and pumas and hantavirus rodents. It was desert the Mormons made bloom, not green pastures. And it's not exactly dromedary country, is it? Are camels hoofed, anyway?" (The poor old guy was showing signs of exhaustion: he asked himself questions out loud.)

I tried to bring him back on topic, or at least to the right continent. "I guess buffalo are out these days."

"Since time is not of the essence, Tommy, maybe you could wait for a giant asteroid to come along and knock our planet out of kilter, just enough to adjust our backyard into a clime and latitude more appropriate for the harvesting of animal jelly. Such as Brazil. I always thought tapirs would make nice gelatin. Kind of amber-colored."

Dad got dreamy for a second. He was getting mature on me. It was downright foreboding. The day would come when I'd have to say goodbye to this old soul.

"Dad? Hey, Dad, how about small inoffensive animals? Would the feet of small inoffensive animals yield this dreck?

Like, could I render appreciable amounts from Tiffany's cat? What if I were to be conscientious about pulling out its claws by the roots every time it comes to defile our glass works?"

"Assuming cat claws can produce gelatin, which they most definitely cannot, sure, why not?" he said, ambiguously enough.

After a brief, silent moment of shared puzzlement, Dad decided it might be better to clarify the question a bit further. It was decided that I could cause Tiffany Jacobsen to have a birthday party with a rental Shetland pony, whose little feet I could mutilate, then dole out the residue, pickled or jerked, to my niter miners and hut rotators as a treat to forefend that general strike. I'd entice the creature to the redwood fence with a fistful of velvety, fragrant clover, or whatever constituted our lawn.

On TV was a violent silent, eyes poked out and heads cracked open with billiard balls. The star did some authentic juggling and instigated a revolting mud fight, which metastasized gradually to encompass a whole neighborhood and scores of strange-looking people, including a dozen Bradleyesque pituitary cases.

"And grab a pygmy pony foot or two—"

"With a snare—"

"Contrived of plaited tendrils—"

"Of course."

"—and tear the hooves off."

"With one's teeth—"

"None left. Sacrificed for the emulsion."

"My father and I are one," says Jesus in the gospel of his beloved disciple. Mine and I were getting carried away—no, galloping off together, united under a yoke of hereditary lawlessness.

"Hack the hoofs free from pinto ankles with a crude stone implement."

"Dislodge a flagstone from the patio. Crudely bonk it against the foundation till you get a jaggedy edge for sawing."

"Yeah. Dislodge all the flagstones. Scatter them. Grind the Nancy-boy charcoal underfoot. Fuck the screenplay."

"Language!" cried Dad.

Frowning dutifully, he made a two-handed move like a symphonic conductor urging a diminuendo. The television cooperated, quite coincidentally. After the messy orgasm of the mud fight, the on-screen activities were getting a little calmer. The Bradley grizzlies were coaxed off-screen with chunks of raw pork. Some crude exposition was being laid down, in preparation for the next access of post-Gold Rush bestiality.

"That pony," Dad reminded us both, "comes all the way from the Shetland Islands."

"Damn. That's right."

"I mean, the Shets, or whoever, speak English. I guess. But that's still way, way out. Ultima Thule. Long way from the old backyard you know so well."

"Adulterative," I agreed, and cast about desperately some more. I was on the verge of wondering out loud whether LaMar Jacobsen's fingernails might be in any useful way similar to the homologous bits on horses and cows, when our eyes met, and I knew Dad was having the same thought, or one equally impermissible, even for a Bradley.

Well, it should come as no surprise that my father and I came very close that morning, on moral grounds, to an outright rejection of gelatin as a recourse. Animal products carried too many implications. And glass itself wound up faring not much better.

"Hold on, son. Let's just say, for argument's sake, that you and I somehow managed to cough up copious amounts of primo animal jelly. And we got the images onto glass. It would have to be a pretty remarkable glass, wouldn't it? Not just bubbly, cat-shitty melted sand. And the frame rate would be ridiculously low, about one and a half per second. Say we were able to sneak a pinch or two of manganese in there. Still, any glass the likes of us could fabricate in such a place as our backyard would probably show a fatal tendency to shatter, even at that snail's pace. So we're talking really jerky picture quality here. Make old Harold Lloyd look like little Miss Seen Yer Hynie, or whatever that curly-headed skater's name was. We'd provide our audience with barely the illusion of the motion that gives motion pictures that certain moving quality from which movies take their mobile name, if you take the hint. It would be more like 'Pictures at an Exposition' for easily bored people."

"Glass pretty much sucks, doesn't it, Dad?"

"That it does."

He was primed and ready. I would try again with the unhallowed preparation. It was getting too late in the day for emotional blackmail to be necessary. I remained cheerful and spoke frankly. For the third time (and you know how often things have to happen in fairy tales and dirty jokes), I asked him, "So what's the name of that plasticky—"

"Hey, I thought kids these days were supposed to be lazy. Why are you making everything so difficult? Why do you need to produce and direct and shoot your own? Don't I drive you downtown whenever some Walt Disney pig-and-rat show comes around?"

"—stuff they use for film?"

Theretofore he'd succeeded in distracting me. But now I'd gone and said the F-word. Supportive, kind and gentle, and liberal, he didn't want to nip a young person's dream in the bud. He didn't want to pee on my parade. But—

"Celluloid?" he gasped. He sighed. Or did my father moan? I hope he didn't whimper; in any case, I refuse to depict him doing so.

"We need something see-through, and we're agreed that glass bites, right, Dad?"

"Are you sure you've received a true vocation for the cinema? Is this going to be like the bass clarinet and the ham radio? You don't really like movies that much, do you?"

He knew very well what my future slaves must never find out (particularly the males among them): that I secretly preferred reading—with the exception of *The Swiss Family Robinson*, which is a genuinely vile book in every respect.

But, in prosperous countries, youngsters must be given, must be force-fed, if necessary, the opportunity and the wherewithal to pursue even their most fleeting and halfhearted interests. These are little human beings forming themselves, after all. Just that year I'd already gone through astronomy, cartooning, sandal making, ventriloquism (lessons mail-ordered from the back pages

of a *Sergeant Rock* funny book) and the cello. If such an institution had existed back then, Father would have offered to mortgage
the house and send me to film school after I got myself expelled
from the publicly funded Mormon seminary-in-disguise, if I'd only let him go to work in the meantime.

"For celluloid I'll need, obviously, cellulose."

"Obtainable from trees or little boys' cotton underpants,"
came Dad's muffled words. In dejection he had folded his leg-
long arms into an ostrich-sized nest and buried his head. He
moaned, "And you've just got to have some alcohol, I suppose.
There's something fermentable out there, don't you fret, Tommy.
But no drinky-winky."

Even without being able to see his face, I could tell there
was something else. Those mammoth shoulders shuddered at the
very idea of the unnamed stuff. He tried to tuck it deep as a he-
morrhoid pad, presumably for later, in case he hadn't succeeded in
putting his son off creativity altogether in the interim. Dad unbu-
ried his head, for there was an announcement to be made.

"Coming by the third ingredient for primitive plastics
manufacture is going to be a problem, kid. The third ingredient,
I'm afraid, given the perimeters and parameters you've established
for yourself—"

"Who said I established them for myself?"

"—is flat-ass impossible. It doesn't grow here."

"Oh, so it's a plant. Wow, old man, you really tipped your
hand there. Blabbermouth."

"It's plant-derived. And, as far as I can see, the only absolutely insurmountable obstacle to your directorial debut would be
the irremediable absence of this particular type of vegetation from
our backyard. Not in a thousand years could you grow that here in
our Rocky Mountain enclave."

"Why not? What about a million or two?"

"Well, boy, given that sort of time frame, our backyard
has been under ice, under sea water, and is sort of half-assed desert
now. But I really doubt it was ever sufficiently like those locales
in the Far East where the camphor tree grows. There, I said it: the
camphor tree. And it is by no means a cosmopolitan organism...
at least I don't think it is." He glanced toward the book room.

My reluctance to resort to that place heartened Father, and supplied him with confidence in the accuracy of his point. In fact, he felt triumph coming on, and the sensation made him wax a tad grandiloquent. The ostrich nest was dismantled, and he began to beat the air with vast wings.

"Yes, think of the unfathomably intricate combinations and permutations of pollinators and predators and so forth required to nurture even a normal type of tree—"

"And how much more so," I reluctantly concurred, "a weird-ass one that you can sniff and clear the snot out of your nose."

"It also chases moths away. Do you reckon, young Tommy, the necessary far-eastern camphor tree-friendly things could occur, all at once, in perfect concert, here in the Far West? Old Mother Earth wobbles on her axis, but not that much."

Dad went even further and pointed out the historical unavailability of camphor in the entire western hemisphere. "That, no doubt, explains why the Greeks never discovered plastic. They harnessed steam, for toys, and invented the notion of coin-op. But not celluloid." He paused, looked at the bakelite clock cellophane-taped to the polyvinyl-chloride wallpaper, and muttered, as an aside—certainly not to me, and maybe not even to himself (did he hear himself say it?), "Thank God Almighty."

Was he, or was he not, capitalizing the substantive? Was he thinking of the implications, in the context of our confab that morning? Almost definitely not. It's too late to ask him now.

"Turn the old Greeks loose with a source of camphor wood," he mused, "and we'd be sitting on two and a half millennia's worth of brightly-colored, incorruptible shit, instead of just a century's."

"Hey, that's right!" I was even more eager to proceed now that I understood my efforts might remain everlasting. "Maybe something close enough to camphor grew here at one time, in the New World, right where our backyard is now. The Utes couldn't be expected to—well, you know."

Dad looked at the clock again, but with a different sort of expression this time. "Would have to be millions and zillions, positive Sagans of years ago," he anachronized.

"If then."

And we looked at each other and said, in unison, "But, so what?"

"Time's no problem. Like that Eternal Thingamabob you were teaching me."

"Recurrence," said Dad. "Eternal Recurrence."

We were now officially no longer even pretending to be scientific. This shift in mode of discourse was certainly heralded or accompanied by a parallel escalation in Mack Sennet's special effects. But I don't recall what that might've involved, dream images being hard to keep in your head over time.

Suppertime had rolled around, followed by a discolored sunset over the dead sea, and the madman at the Mormon TV station was still displaying his sepia shorts, sans commercial interruption. Dad and I had not only forgotten about his job, but about nourishing our bodies, as we continued this duel literally to the death. Now it was just a matter, also literally, of materials, finite, and a question of the spatial boundaries of my system, self-imposed, self-circumscribed—for we had dispensed with temporal restraints once and for all, and entered the realm of the Eternal Recurrence.

This was a further step in the program of my "corruption" at Father's hands. He had given me Eternal Recurrence as ammunition, to stow in my arsenal alongside Darwinism, for salvos against the "Elder," that bristly indoctrinator of the Latter-Day-Saints' world-view and faith, who, salaried with state tax money, thinly masqueraded as my homeroom teacher at the neighborhood public school. I was equipped with Eternal Recurrence for use as a further prod, a second prick, as it were, to torment the Mormon educator, just in case I ever succeeded in getting him to engage me on even more cosmological questions than the origin of species. I hadn't, yet, gotten him to engage me, but had retained this peculiar doctrine in the back of my head, where, evidently, it had been percolating and depositing layers of something or other in the fatty synaptic clefts of my central nervous system.

The idea, bluntly, is as follows: the way God, or the Demiurge, or whoever, would build, say, a car would be to take the components and throw them against a wall again and again, over and over, for however long it took for those nuts and bolts to fall accidentally into the right places to produce a car. He's got time. No efficient assembly lines for him. Henry Ford was no child of this unhurried crapshooter deity.

Dad would always drawl it out, "Gaw-w-wd the Faw-w-w-wther," in such a way that I could feel the quotation marks like fishhooks. This was definitely not the guy the "Elder" groveled to and praised so piously in pseudo-science class. Not a regular sort of guy at all. For example, he didn't appear to have a whole lot of personality. In this way, Dad's god resembled LaMar Jacobsen.

Along with atoms crapped sans surcease against the wall, came irrefutably the concomitant notion that the backyard, and Dad, and Tiffany's cat, and even (unlikely as it may sound) little Tommy, right along with everything else, would eventually happen not just once, but again and again, infinite numbers of times, over the course of eternity—-for, if the atoms fell in these particular configurations once, what's to stop them doing so again? Dad assured me this was an idea tailor-made to irk the ire of any mainstream Utahn with the basic intellect to grasp it.

Only later in life did I learn this doctrine was the self-same Eternal Recurrence that tortured Nietzsche and tickled Schiller. I suspect cheerful Schiller was Dad's source, assuming he had a source, and didn't independently arrive at this conclusion—which seems so obvious and inevitable and common-sensical, once your brain's been exposed to it.

We were both assuming, like those two fine old Krauts of yore, that the process was restricted to currently available matter, such stuff budgeted from day one, shuffled and jumbled but undestroyed if not uncreated. God was grounded in a backyard, too, with a fence.

"But," asked Tommy, "how do we know matter is finite?"—and answered his own idiotic question with another question before the former completely exited his mouth. Do you see a density as of lead between the surface of your corneas and Alpha Centauri? Matter is palpably finite.

I was too young, and my father was too late for work, to broach the horrible subject of the identity of energy and matter, and the recent theories of time, which limit and bend its duration in very messy ways. But it wasn't as though the "Elder" would be prepared to throw these in my face by way of refutation. My homeroom was a nineteenth-century time capsule, and there was no need to hit the book room and arm myself with the latest conceits—which tend to be no fun, anyway.

Eternal Recurrence would be just the thing, my father evidently thought, to drive the Latter-Day-Saints wacky all the way and get me expelled altogether. Darwin was only good for suspensions—but this was dynamite. I, on the other hand, doubted the idea could be introduced into my homeroom teacher's clouded mind with sufficient clarity and completeness to raise so much as a half a hackle. Besides, I didn't think explosive results were guaranteed. I still don't.

It's no weirder than what they're already taught to believe. With a little bit of tinkering here and there, you could probably adjust Eternal Recurrence to jibe more tightly with the Mormon world-view than the Catholic or Protestant (neither of which they share, being an unChristian outfit, despite the posturings of a certain failed presidential candidate).

If you are a Mormon male, and if you discreetly marry and fecundate as many females as you can without going to jail, meanwhile tithing faithfully off the top every month "without stint or surcease," and if, via the conduit of your plural spouses, you bring down to earth a grotesquely large contingent of the finite number of pre-created souls from heaven, or whatever repository they are stored in (my nephew Shawn never clarified this point for me), and if you baptize them into the Utah church and teach them to tithe—then, upon death, you will become a Mormon god yourself, and be furnished with, not merely your own backyard, but your own planet, and a harem of secret, eternal, nameless wives, upon whom to get souls with which to populate that planet, who will tithe, and tithe, and continue to tithe still more, and so on ad infinitum.

It seems to me that the metaphor of a perpetual crapshoot could be substituted with a semen shoot of comparable duration, and the rest of Mormonism would fall right into place.

Considering his modus operandi, it's unlikely that Gaw-w-w-wd himself, even with the full recruitment and cooperation of the Church of Jesus Christ of Latter-Day-Saints, could make a movie in my backyard without starting all over again, shooting that stuff against the wall, constituting and reconstituting the universe until some really big asteroid congeals in a previously unoccupied cranny of our solar system, and swings along and busts the fuck out of earth, knocking us entirely out of kilter, so that, as my father said—

"Up becomes down, this becomes that, the first shall be the last, and so on. Except this time you'll have to make arrangements for it to clobber us even harder than it did when sending us to animal jelly latitudes. It'll have to whack us silly until our backyard gets relocated all the way over to the Orient, where the snot-zapper tree grows. But I wouldn't count on that happening real soon. It's very unlikely. It's not the sort of thing a good manager is eager to factor into his timetable. And I assume we want to bring this project in under budget. Jesus Christ, kid. Instead of waiting around for this rogue heavenly body to tumble us ass-over-tea-kettle behind the Bamboo Curtain, wouldn't it be a skosh more efficient to just get on your bike and go down to the drug store and get a box of fucking camphor? I'll front you the bread, man."

(He frequently used beatnik lingo when trying to persuade me, thinking it sounded youthful and hip enough to get through. Not even my big brother fell for it any more.)

I said, "Nope, fuck that," or the little-boy equivalent thereof, and stopped listening.

My unconsidered, hardly verbalized, congenitally prewired instinct told me, if you're going to bother to get off your lackadaisical Bradley ass and actually do something (which by no means was a requirement in those prosperous days of my boyhood's America, where white folks like me, even non-Mormons stuck in "Zion," were owed a living on account of our external characteristics), then you should make it something you can do yourself, alone, from scratch, no shopkeepers or midwives or pimps or pinsetters involved. Collaboration dilutes, renders maculate. It's not the American way.

And why throw yourself and your budget of non-renewable energy/matter into something that requires a whole military-industrial complex, backed up by a world-wide distribution network, just to gather the basic materials to bring it into existence? My great-great auntie managed to invent her private language eight hundred miles away from the nearest railroad track.

One of the requisites for making a movie came from elsewhere, down the block at the drug store. The asteroid that might bring it closer was not exactly sizzling on the horizon. And the whole point was that no ingredient must be alien or extraneous to our perimeters; each constituent must stay within certain redwood boundaries. This strange process had to be topographically circumscribed, as part of the discipline, the decorum. On that day—though neither Bradley was more than dimly aware of it—our backyard was nothing less than the self. Whole and individuated, quadrilateral and topiaried, it was the archetypal walled garden of the soul.

So, rather than allow his virginal soul to be sullied, rendered maculate, was little Tommy finally ready to throw in the directorial towel? Did he really mean it when he said that other F-word a minute ago? It's not as though he would be alone in acquiescing. Even Dad seemed to think the time for fucking it had finally arrived.

"You've got problems, kid. Glass plates would shatter, and there can be none of the proverbial celluloid, probably, and your world premiere is permanently postponed—if you can talk of permanence, which you can't. I'm afraid your production has hit a wall, and it's never going to bounce back in one piece, no matter how many times you ram your little head into the bricks. No silver screen magic, not even moldy bark magic, in suburban Salt Lake City, at least not this time around in the cycle of Eternal Etcetera. This sort of thing happened to Orson Welles all the time. He learned some card tricks and just got on with his life. And he has been hailed as an authentic American genius. Can I go to work now? It's almost time for me to start heading home—that is, if I want to get my usual jump on the return rush hour and make it back here in time to spend some quality time with you before beddy-bye, as a good daddy ought. Goom-bye please?"

In the elemental face of all this, with the Father and the Universe both refusing to cooperate, did little Tommy dig deep into himself and somehow muster the wherewithal to persevere? Don't you know he did? This is what they mean when they talk about the tenacity of youth.

I buttonholed my dad just as he stooped to make it through the door and, this time, with nothing but a plucky little facial expression, blocked the former basketball pro. My feat was all the more impressive because it was dark now and neither of us had switched on the lights. The flicker of primitive celluloid transmogrified into rudimentary pixels was all we had to see each other by.

The congenital subnormals had been allowed back into the picture, and were getting vaguely organized. A contingent of the Bradleyesque pituitary goons was on the verge of gaining the upper hand. They restarted the mud fight and escalated immediately to rocks.

"The asteroid belt," I whispered, "is a flying Rocky Mountain range. It's only a matter of time."

Dad looked at me for an indeterminate while. Then he sighed with all the reluctance of a general who's decided to go nuclear. He sat back down.

"Okay, okay," he said. "We've loitered out there for a hefty segment of geologic time, and the blackjack of Jehovah has come along and given us a planetary subcranial concussion. And east has met west, up has become down, this that, first last. Wonder of wonders, camphor is growing in the backyard. We have a whole fucking forest of nasal decongestant, and bags and bags of celluloid, more than enough to make about eighteen sequels to *Lawrence of Arabia*. Now, boy, are you ready for the hardest question of all?"

"Does a fat dog fart?"

I sat up straight and flipped my Beatle bangs out of my eyes, ready. In the silent short subject, a two-story frame house was being razed to the ground by the bare hands of a gigantic man with a lopsided face.

"What about your actors, son?"

I don't recall if he'd already given me the embarrassing speech about the Birds and the Bees and the Condoms (sturdy latex—none of this farm critter intestine tripe). I don't think he had.

The received wisdom in those days was to hold that speech off till your child started smelling bad. That malodorous moment was also the signal for parents to start allowing dates with the opposite sex. I hadn't started smelling bad yet, I'm sure of that—though my olfactory memory can't claim the sharpness of Proust's gustatory. In any case, I was not prepared for Dad's question at all. I thought Lassie was a boy and Bambi the opposite. Little Tommy, while "borderline precocious" in certain ways, was a perfect latency-period sexual cipher, like a 'droid in some cheap sci-fi flick of a slightly later time.

Yes, in this respect, I was a typical doomed preadolescent, deep in the pre-genital phase, if you want to get all psychoanalytical. In other words (not to sugar-coat it or anything), I hadn't quite started "beating the brains out of Charles the Bald," as the French intellectuals like Derrida and Foucalt like to say and do in print. But I'd reluctantly heard naughty talk at school, and wasn't eager to be subjected to more at home, from my own dad, yet. It was far too icky.

"What about my actors?" I said in an innocent-sounding tone, trying to deflect the paternal will and impulse. "Well, I'll feed them on crab apples just like my slaves."

"You know I'm not talking about commissary privileges now. I assume you want full artistic control of this flick as well as every other kind of control. You want to decide absolutely everything, right down to the genetic makeup of your performers, right?"

"Gee-whiz, Dad. I honestly never—"

Tongue-tied, I looked to the TV for moral support, and saw great aunties and second cousins-once-removed, all botched. Control should have been exerted over their
coming into being.

"Given, Tommy, a nice little twig-and-tendril lean-to for privacy back there, and the proper, shall we say, management techniques, you could probably come up with just those characteristics your little heart desires: the cheekbones and the precise shade of turquoise irises, the vocal cords and muscles, or lack thereof, and even, depending on where you stand on Nature versus

Nurture, the personality traits dramatically called for in your script. You are using a script—?"

"Charcoal on the flagstones. Like you said."

"I thought we scattered the flagstones."

"I just gathered them back up."

"And didn't we grind the charcoal underfoot?"

"I gathered that back up, too."

This was getting altogether too heuristic, even for little Tommy. It was little Tommy's turn to demur, to put the brakes on, to introduce restraints. Maybe step back a bit and scribble out a preliminary scenario, to see where we're headed before we get in too deep. Engage the alphabet, effeminate though it may be, before we start churning out the bodily fluids. Little Tommy cleared his throat and asked, "How much time are we talking about here, Dad?"

"Time? What does time matter? We're in Mormon heaven now, and you're the boss. It's your planet we're peopling."

Unfortunately, this was in the days before human genetic engineering oozed off the pages of the trash novels and into actual labs. In any case, I'm sure we didn't have the time, that dwindling day, to determine whether I could scratch and scrounge up the necessary pyrex and agar (which comes from seaweed, a definite no-have in the Mormon "Zion"). We were stuck, in that dim epoch, with old-fashioned, messy selective breeding. Now I understood his earlier cryptic comment about a special use for Tiffany Jacobsen. She was too chubby. The thought was very off-putting.

So little Tommy, all by himself, came up with what he considered the only truly insuperable stymie to his homespun Hollywood hopes. And what would that stymie be? It would be Dad's sick-making idea of doing it in the backyard, people dorking behind twig-and-tendril lean-to's, with girls. Gross. Cooties.

It only occurred to me later, in adulthood (about three seconds ago, as a matter of fact), to wonder if Dad was thinking about asking me to film the kiddies doing it. Forget that, you sick old prick.

He did, however, have an excellent point, which was not to be ignored. My actors would be my screen personae, the various aspects and attributes of *me* that I presented to the world in my

art. Was I going to let their lineaments be determined by god
knew what Utah-style miscegenation, what unconsidered polygamist inbreeding, these very creatures whose images the fore-
going rigmarole had been essayed to capture? I should say not.
Besides, I didn't want Dad to think I was a homo, an invert-sugar.
He wasn't getting my gonads that easily.

So, no turd-burglar, I managed to swallow the nausea of
my own first sexual flusterment, and choke out a tiny, "Okay," to
which Dad replied with a double take and an audible gasp. He'd
thought he had me by the bicuspids this time. He'd been counting
the fillings, like a concentration camp commandant.

"We're talking about many, many generations here," he
reminded me. I detected an edge of desperation in his manner.
He'd already lost a day's work, so that wasn't what made him
twitch now with an evident urge to dive out the front door.

His present discomfiture notwithstanding, he knew better
than to ask me outright if I had a problem with the multi-
generational thing. A question of personal immortality is the
wrong one to ask a full-blooded American elementary school boy
with no special needs or professionally diagnosed learning disabil-
ities or alternate sexual orientations to speak of, as yet. The answer you're going to get is, "Forever. Just like you, Dad. I'm
immortal. It runs in the Bradley family. Must be a recessive gene.
Time's no problem."

And yet, of course, in spite of my brave affirmation (and I
only imitated my father), it was the point of death I was uncons-
ciously considering this whole time, even at that tender age. Maybe Father was, also, at his no less tender age, despite his own asse-
verations to the contrary, pondering that ultimate moment, when
the things you can't take with you when you go, are gone, and
you're on your own for real, rattling and gasping away in a
doomed declaration of independence, with hardly any help, then
no help at all, then outright hindrance, from your heart and lungs
and so forth.

What I was ready to dig so deep for in the backyard dirt
was that self-sustaining system which we all wind up embodying
so briefly at the end-time. I was looking forward, in the back of
my prepubescent, self-absorbed brain, to demise and disengage-

ment, when girls and the icky cooties they bring couldn't be more irrelevant. The child is father to the man, and the pre-teen forebear to the corpse.

I scrounged back there for utter autonomy, which (for a non-Mormon at any rate) can only come with the precise arrival of death: the sole moment of pure freedom, mortal coil successfully shuffled off at last, after a lifetime of squirming. And this freedom continues—who knows how long? Probably about the duration of a short subject illuminated by a pinch of magnesium. And it feels, no doubt, a lot like nitrous oxide recreationally administered to excess.

My father, the self-proclaimed "immortal," achieved that fleeting liberty eight months ago, as I'm sure you knew he was going to do—we all must kill our fathers eventually. I kept my teeth, not to mention my balls, which means his life had to cease. This is how it's supposed to be.

Just a means of bumping off Dad, this section of the book, I'm making it very explicit. I did it, and you watched. Over the course of this thing I've driven the poor old fart crazy, actually rendered him a dithering maniac at the end, sitting at the kitchen table in the dark, snickering incoherently about a backyard jail-bait stud service, his work torn away from him—that is to say, I murdered my father in the only way that matters. And, up until the paragraph just before this one, most of the Aristotelian unities have been preserved.

"We're talking real primitive here," he says to me at night, sometimes, after I've fallen asleep in front of the television. "You might wind up with shadows hulking on the wall, just ghosts disembodied. Doomed for a certain term to walk the night, and all that sort of thing."

Every month or so they tell us a bit more about what's in outer space, and so far it just sounds like one big hazardous chemical dump. The multitudinous Mormon gods up there are committing the sin of Onan on a very large scale, perpetually spilling their seed on the most barren ground. If the rest of our solar system is any indication, the extra-terrestrial universe must comprise mere worlds with sulfuric acid rain and nitrous oxide atmospheres, maybe a squalid wretch of a microscopic worm here and there, more mud than life—but mostly this toxic idiocy, repeated over and over in the context of billions and quadrillions of galaxies and so on.

That sounds to me like just about the right number of trial runs and abortive attempts and false starts it would take, throwing a limited number of atoms against the wall for an unlimited period, to produce, this time around, what's coiled and tucked so neatly behind my personal eyeballs and between my Bradley ear-holes.

And no matter how bored this crapshooting Jupiter got trying to toss up the next version of me, he couldn't very well get on his bicycle and go down to the drug store and get a box of Bradley molecules to help him fudge a bit, speed things up a skosh, not any more than I could have fetched that box of imported camphor, now could he? Not very likely, I'd say.

However, just a few hours ago, with the aid of the internet, I discovered that camphor trees from China and Japan do indeed grow in the western hemisphere. They were imported to the U.S.A. about a hundred years ago, not too long after a certain clan of hyperextended coal miners arrived from Sheffield, England. And they (the trees, not us) are multiplying like weeds, to the detriment of native life forms. The *cinnamomum camphora* is choking out whole forests in Florida, where it is subject to no natural predators. Introduced as a garden ornament, it's now registered among the Category One pest species.

There was a camphor tree, in fact, unbeknownst to the Bradleys (neither being a botanist), rankly sprouting a few feet beyond Tiffany Jacobsen's mom's crab apple tree, just out of reach. The asteroid would've only had to nudge us about ten yards in that direction. I might have made my contribution to world cinema after all, but for that groundless, ill-informed, careless, facile parental discouragement. A waste irrecoverable, a loss immeasurable for human culture. Besides, I'm told that turpentine would have worked almost as well.

But, on that day of my early youth, which won't come again (at least not this time around), the unavailability of celluloid's third ingredient was presented to me as an insurmountable stymie, and rubbed in my little face, right along with the simple fact of my constitutional inability to do what it took to exert deox-

Tom Bradley

yribonucleic control over my performers. So I said, "Fuck it," and became a novelist instead.

I immersed myself in the sissy-pants alphabet, and, with that single stroke of fearless will, obviated most of the problems discussed in this section of the book. I confess I have no idea where the graphite in my pencil comes from, but it could, with extra effort, instead be charcoal from my dad's unpopular black locust—if that trash tree hadn't died of aphids or something and rotted to nothing about twenty-five years ago.

Now I'm writing one, not about a boy and his old pappy in a backyard, but about a pair of stumblers across the length and breadth of the entire world as known and unknown at a certain circumscribed epoch in the relatively distant past. It involves a lot of research, and the books I'm using come from everywhere, and are made from every bookish substance.

Dad's last words were actually crooned: "I'm checkin' out, goom-bye." And, before he did that, I borrowed his library card and did some checkin'-out and goom-byeing myself: nearly 200 books taken far away across the Pacific Ocean in suitcases, to the lands of the camphor tree, where I now languish in economic exile, having long ago been deemed too unsocialized even for the non-Mormon university back home. Father's program of son-corruption succeeded beyond his dreams.

Yes, I confess that I put a hideous number of items on his account, and he croaked in the meantime. My big brother goes around telling everybody back home that the first overdue notice killed him with shock.

God knows what glues, what gelatins, what larval wor-mlets, what inorganic compounds and artificial dyes I've intro-duced into the ecosystem of my far-oriental hovel. Books from places like Bombay and Holland and Oklahoma State University, some from another century, and now a new millennium (if you're prepared to overlook Dennis the Lesser's miscalculation).

Even though the Chinese say "Stealing books is not steal-ing," I would not want any astronomical overdue fines tallied against his reverend name in the Golden Register Up Yonder. So I renew these babies' checkout status every two months, by transoceanic fax, with his immemorial name and social security number ball-pointed, immutable, at the top of the sheet.

But the date is buried a half-dozen times per year under another layer of liquid paper, progressively thicker and thicker, composed of lamp black and mustard oil, which would have been easy to manage in my backyard, but also methylcyclohexane, vinyl toluene-butadiene copolymer, dioctyl sodium, titanium dioxide sulfosuccinate, not to mention vinyl toluene-butadiene copolymer, plus isobutyl methacrylate and—hard as it may be to believe—n-butyl methacrylate.

See how far I am now from that boyish fantasy? See what remains of my ambition to build a natural economy to parallel that of my outcast pioneer ancestors in their Rocky Mountain caves? I have to employ all these outré essences and quintessences just to get my novels written.

Every two months I personally account for a quantum rise in the world-wide consumption of polymeric fatty ester, alkyds, cyclohexa-nedimethanol (I feel particularly guilty about that one), pentaerythritol, phthalate, certain coumarone-indene resins sold under the trade-name Neville, and, most mortifying of all, dioctyl sodium sulfosuccinate as well as bistridecyl sodium sulfosuccinate.

My closed system is falling apart with a vengeance here, as I sink deeper into material promiscuity, substance abuse, layer by layer, until my check-out renewal form can barely be crammed into the fax machine anymore. A technology, already dated and idiotically simple in principle (snot, available by the quart in any red-blooded American boy's backyard, would do almost the same thing), reveals my multiple chemical dependence, my adulterous nature. We don't remain for long unsustained from without.

We have (or need to believe we have) an undying dad, our perpetual victualler. And, for the purposes of this piece of nonfiction, I had to quell my grief long enough to adjust my own victualler's passing into non-perpetuity. I knew I would have either to kill Father off much longer ago than the actual half-month that marks the short-term anniversary of his death today, or else cause the Salt Lake City Public Library circulation department to require renewal faxes at the unreasonable rate of every day or so, in order for the accumulation of liquid paper to get egregious enough to warrant such an elaborate image in a nonfiction book of this particular length.

I can encompass and re-schedule the death of a minor sports figure, but am impotent to arrest my own descent into technological whoredom. Liquid paper is only the flaky epidermis of my Karloffian organism of corruption. I shudder to think what was required to bring this book to your eyes, simply pencil-scrawled though it might have been in the original: the interlinkage of contrivances that no single person could build from scratch, no matter how borderline-precocious his brain, how big his backyard, or indulgent his father.

Account has been taken of Einstein's temporal relativism. The signals of the email message to which these words were attached traveled so far at the speed of light that the newfangled wishy-washy time was obliged to slow down for them. After bouncing off whatever communications satellite hovers over the Pacific between here and there, they arrived on the surface of America too late, even though the whole transaction was instantaneous. (Figure that one out with a prepubescent brain full of *The Swiss Family Robinson*.) The receiving dish in Kansas or wherever was necessarily nudged just the right distance toward my modem in East Asia, to compensate for the earth's rotation that we, but not my ideas, lived through in the meantime. Thanks to the account taken of this newly enfeebled fourth dimension, my words were prevented from swishing right past you—and thus is illegitimized the very basic assumption of all: the immutability (and hence purely unproblematical nature) of time. Time, it turns out, is indeed a problem.

My ultimate act of unfiliality, of Dad-betrayal, is not his murder, but rather the practical negation of the doctrine he taught me for my self-preservation. How can you have Eternal Recurrence when time is compressed and stretched like poorly rendered animal jelly? Eternity itself becomes a non-sequitur, "recurrence" an oxymoron, the moment you blur the distinction between then and now.

So I'm left with no secret weapon against the "Elders" of this world. I might as well kiss ten percent of my income goodbye, undo my belt, and just let go, backslide. I should sign up for baptism into the faith that nearly wiped us Bradleys out long ago.

Until that ultimate succumbing, I whittle my Ticonderoga 2.5 to what may be a compulsive degree, so the point where my enthusiasms scrape the paper will remain almost geometrically circumscribed, a contact that will be easiest to disengage when the time for disengagement comes.

A Pleasure Jaunt with One of the Sex Workers Who Don't Exist in the People's Republic of China

Take away the prostitutes from human affairs,
and you'll throw everything into a chaos of lusts.
—Saint Augustine, De Ordine ii, 4

Sam Edwine and his presumably contagion free rent-a-date were being Red Flag Limousined through the very mountain forests where, in times gone by, Coxinga the Pirate once paused to hold a funeral for his baby, knowing he'd be overtaken and wiped out.

It was impossible to tell whether the chauffeur was smiling unkindly through the rearview mirror at Sam's cramped knees and low pigmentation. Despite the sweat guzzling heat and humidity, the guy had covered the lower half of his face with one of those white surgical masks affected by Asians with colds or halitosis, real or imagined.

How could this operator of heavy machinery have known in advance that the whore was bringing her little greasy balls of poppy tar? And, if he had known, why hadn't he felt compelled, in his capacity as the joy-ride's on-board representative of the provincial government, to blow the whistle on the tart, instead of merely taking passive measures to protect his own mouth and nose from the seductive fumes? And why hadn't he brought a mask for Sam?

The mosquitoes were so big they had body odor. The liters of plasmatic fluid they'd already drained from Sam's ankles, combined with the mollifying effects of the second-hand smoke (thick as fudge mousse in the back seat), caused famous Thumbelina Edwine to comport herself suitably in her nest of orange curls. No problem down there behind Sam's zipper.

"It only takes one sperm cell, one god, one editor," he babbled out the window.

And, just as the sun was beginning to set, the tunnel of deciduous trees crumbled like socialist concrete and they came to the gate of a village, languishing in a remote quadrant of subtropical nowhere. The central authorities rented time on Israeli spy satellites to photograph places like this, in order to determine, for the first time in forty centuries, just how many population centers China might have. Tax purposes, no doubt.

As no roads capable of accommodating this tank circumvented it, the chauffeur was forced to penetrate the peculiar hamlet, but with a reluctance severe enough to be interesting. He asked Sam to close the black velvet drapes and sit back, ignorant and passive, until they came to the exit on the other side.

That, of course, only piqued curiosity further. Could this village be the reason why the whole mountain was declared off-limits? Sam determined that the curtains must be kept open, just a slit. Like Odysseus persuading his boys to tie him to the mast, Sam offered the man behind the wheel a pack of the best Flower and Willow Lane Winstons, purloined fresh from his fellow passenger's black sequined handbag while she nodded off. He further predisposed the driver in his favor by calling him shifu.

"Don't worry," said Sam, pulling his outsized custom-made Lenin cap down by way of camouflage. "I'm an old China hand. I understand the delicate situation perfectly. The cops are always begging my honorable patron, your honorable boss, to keep me under wraps when I go downtown, because my sheer manly beauty causes traffic jams, like one of those anarcho-syndicalistic thingies, and—"

"This is not the same thing. Not at all."

"Oh, come off it. The mug's not that hideously pale. Is it?"

But there was something very close to fear in the soldier's eyes (for that's what he was: regular People's Liberation Army all the way). Maybe fear was on his lips, too. Red spots began to soak through the white fabric of his mask, indicating that the twin sirloins were being nervously gnawed upon. So Sam not only said okay, but meant it. For now, anyway.

The village gatekeeper skittered out of his tiny sentry box and snarled like a terrier. Like his counterparts stationed in front of every walled compound in the country, he was a territorial critter, and would piss on your hydrant if you didn't take charge and piss on his first.

This uppity guy was the reason why most high- and even middle-level cadres cause their chauffeurs to be armed. The requisite hardware is not tucked under the death seat to foil counterrevolutionary assassins, but to curb these canine gatekeepers, who are made aware, through some unimaginable Pavlovian means, of exactly what types of limo come standard-equipped with Kalashnikov assault rifles.

No need for the passenger inside a Red Flag to roll down the window and state his business, nor to court snarling three-headed Cerberus by calling him shifu, or "master," while sowing at his feet an armload of snacks from the on-board ice chest, such as the black and bitter Cadbury chocolate bars with the phony French name that starts with a B, specially provided by Sam's honorable patron-sugar daddy at the Foreign Affairs Ministry. Sam had no intention of sharing his yummies with anybody. The Blessed Virgin could manifest herself and offer to blow him for a bite—she was welcome to try.

At first he wondered what all the anxiety was about. It seemed to be a ghost town (one of the few things you could imagine that were impossible in China). There was nobody from whom to conceal his questionable face, just dilapidated shops and houses that would have been boarded up in a country less lumber-poor. Grey stucco, death, emptiness: it was just like Sam's part of the world, minus tumbleweeds.

There was one element in the scene that stuck in his eye like a chunk of foreign matter. He looked, then looked again, and was sure he saw one of the best street drainage systems he'd come across south of the Yangtze River. Lining the edges of the avenue which the car was so isolatedly moseying down were actual gutters, clearly surveyed beforehand and executed with excellent concrete, the better to serve as definite channels for whatever fluids might run off the sidewalks and street.

The logical positivist in him tried to ask the whore if she saw them, too; but she didn't seem to grasp the question, for Sam had never learned the dialect word that might distinguish the idea of gutter from the idea of street or floor or toilet. The driver was anxious enough about letting Sam peek out, so it seemed better not to importune him for glosses on the history of this verboten town's civil engineering.

The social history of the absent or invisible burghers, on the other hand, was another matter. It was freely available, and was spewed forth as quickly as it could be improvised.

"They are, shall we say, a national minority. Yes, that's right. Indigenous and so forth. Something not too unlike your Navaho tribesmen, Dr. Edwine. But not so, um, happy. An actual ethnic group is what they are, whom we the Han majority are selflessly trying hard to rehabilitate, reclaim and modernize—"

A point of a white-gloved finger indicated the Han presence in this so far un-peopled community: several P.L.A. regulars manning a long hose on an elephantine tanker truck that slowly approached from a side street. Sam ignored them for now.

"How do those lips taste?" he asked, as yet more scarlet roses bloomed on the surgical mask in the rearview mirror.

Sam's sugar daddy had hired no obtuse chauffeur for tonight's joy ride. Sarcasm didn't necessarily escape him. He flipped his white fingers at an imaginary insect, as if to say, "Who cares what a big-nose like you believes or disbelieves? Nobody, that's who. You're obviously neither a successful capitalist nor one of their pet scribblers, or you would be in Beijing right now getting fat and staying cool, instead of sweating here with me in this pisshole, eating out of a box in the back seat of a superannuated jalopy and considering yourself to be living it up. Nobody will hear you blab about what you're going to see in this place. Even if they did, they wouldn't care enough to believe or disbelieve. You're just a male Anglo Saxon from Utah-zhou, pushing middle age at that.

Your complete, irremediable obscurity is the reason you've been
brought in from the extreme occidental desert to pretend to tutor
the Foreign Affairs Minister, and to kiss his ass for more or less
outrageous favors like tonight. So ask me anything, Dr. Nobody,
and I'll tell you the gods' honest truth, if I happen to feel like it.
Meanwhile, the inmates of this hell will remain whatever the party
says they are."

Sam felt he simply must take exception to that facile ap-
plication of the adjective "irremediable" to his obscurity. And he
wasn't so sure about the "pushing middle age" part, either. It hardly mattered that the unkind words hadn't come from the front seat,
but from his own self-loathing imagination. Some vestigial trace
of self-esteem must have caused Sam's upper body, if not his spirit, to lean forward in the seat, because the driver shouted, "No!
They must not see your face!"

"Who the fuck must not see my—"

Two or three eyes peeped out from behind an overturned
honey wagon halfway down the block. Something too tall stooped
out of a cobwebbed doorway. Three more shambled after, their
skins so unwashed that it was difficult to tell if they were clothed.
The edges of the street began first to twitch, then to writhe as, one
by offputting one, a hobbling mob gathered around the vintage
Red Flag cadre-mobile.

"I saw some of these monsters hanging from the cliffs a
while back!" cried the whore, all perked up now. "They were spy-
ing on us! You know, like monitoring our progress!"

And Sam did recall, at one point in the recent past, craning
his neck at the surrounding mountainsides, his eyes tracing the
vector of an orange and turquoise-crested myna, and seeing something green and rank as vegetation squirm with its own animation
up there. He'd assumed it was the opium inside his eyeballs making things undulate like the draperies in Roderick Usher's parlor.
But now he felt like Siddhartha, exposed to the non-princely world
for the first time.

They followed along behind the car: microcephalics,
mongoloids, every sort of cripple, accompanied by other wretches
less easily categorizable, who gaped and mewled and waved wo-

ven-grass alms bags, their faces contorted with puzzlement over the strange iron creature slithering through their midst.

Sugar Daddy's chauffeur peered hard into the back seat from between a bunch of shampoo-colored plastic grapes festooning the rearview mirror. He observed Sam's eyes as they passed over the scabby heads moiling outside the slit in the black curtains, and fixed on the fringes of the rout. Hanging back there were a few fully grown individuals with normal cephalic indices and frightened, but clear eyes.

"Politically retarded," said the driver. "Ideologically derelict."

Little girls lucky enough to have avoided infanticide took up positions on curbstones fit for an occidental princess, and began to perform. Tiny shell games, card tricks, distressing sorts of gyrations and other potentially profitable behavior combined smoothly with the reflex-motions of lice catching. Some of them lacked digits and other expendable body parts, which had no doubt been removed by Chinese Fagins back in their hometowns to inspire greater generosity and fewer kicks from pedestrians.

The miniature girls didn't expect remuneration from the once-in-a-lifetime cadre mobile. One look in their empty baby eyes revealed that they'd already discounted Sam and his party as a shadow left over from last night's odd dreams. And they didn't cling to the impeccable curbstones for fear of being trampled in the street. Barely heftier than they, and much less agile, the adults posed little threat even to their flaky bones. No, gutter-side shell games and so forth were all they had ever been taught, the extent of their repertoire. Sidewalk gyration was their only reaction to any situation that wasn't immediately life-threatening.

The little whore was delighted. With no strong objections from behind the wheel (anything to draw attention from the large nose that poked between the curtains), she climbed out her window and perched on the hood like a visiting empress in a very short motorcade.

It was permissible for her to view this "indigenous minority," for she was a native and could not possibly unaware of this "ethnic" presence throughout the length and breadth of her motherland (and throughout everybody else's motherland, for that

matter, except maybe the Swiss). Even socialism with Chinese
characteristics couldn't make the inevitable millions of unsociali-
zables disappear. There weren't nearly enough bullets or crematoria at this stage of modernization.

She took off her imported spike heels and let those who
were interested admire her toenails, all reddened by polish, a gift
from Sam, who'd seen the stuff for sale in a joint venture hotel's
deserted gift shop. When some of the less socialized "natives" began to nip at the protein-rich borders of yellow callus, she with-
drew her feet, primly folded them under herself, and got up on
hands and knees, impersonating a hood ornament that some park-
ing lot joker had twisted around ass-backwards.

"The south is red, too!" screamed this working girl, and
reached between her thighs to pull down on the crotch piece of her
acetate drawers. Sam noticed for the first time that her belly was a
bit large. Her arm had to stretch further than might otherwise be
expected.

Maybe the driver was stimulated by his smaller passenger's hooliganism into entertaining thoughts ill-befitting a patriotic
shifu. And perhaps the resultant sensation of guilt that itched behind his red-spotted mask spurred him into recollecting the party
line regarding the whore's clamoring fans. In any case, he began
trying to erase from Sam's memory that momentary lapse into
candor of a few seconds before.

"No, not ideologically derelict. There is no ideology involved here, Dr. Edwine." And he repeated, yet more firmly, "This
is just a particularly backward national minority."

"Bad genes, huh?"

Sam began slipping good things from the ice chest
through the velvet gap, trying to give them the widest possible
angle of dispersion without flashing any physiognomy. Some of
the older and younger ones failed to recognize the packaged deli-
cacies as such; so this muscular Christian decided to unwrap a few
before sowing, and got past half a sandwich before a dinosaur-
sized attack of atavistic late-sixties munchies overtook his narcotic
soaked medulla oblongata. Throughout the ensuing conversation
his mouth was stuffed and restuffed many times over.

"Gene pool murky from inbreeding, huh?" The sarcasm was scarcely muffled by the masses of Heilongjiang cheese that occupied the entire front portion of Sam's head. "That's just like the folks where I come from, who rot in towns not too dissimilar from this, as a matter of fact."

At this point the driver decided that the official mendacity might as well be dispensed with. He sighed, "Before old Deng's advisors cooked up the Internal Resettlement Program, the one thing we were able to pound into their heads—the apolitical heads, I mean—was to run away like madmen, as if their lives depended on it (because their lives did depend on it, if you take my meaning), at the sight or sound or smell of foreigners. Tourists and businessmen are not as morbid as you decadent intelligentsia. They don't travel ten thousand miles to coo over human refuse. So, in the early days of the Open Door Policy, we had a more emphatic way of disposing of the ones who lingered in open cities. And plenty of these, er, people were born with just enough cerebral cortex to remember that time. Your left eyebrow alone, Dr. Edwine, orange as it is, could depopulate this town, which was populated at considerable expense to the People's Republic, and we'll have semi-ambulatory refugees drooling among tea communes in the hills, interfering with the harvest."

The chit-chat seemed about to turn to the inevitable commie topic of production, so boring to a middle-class boy like Sam, whose mom had never allowed him to take summer jobs because they should be saved for the Navahos. He couldn't have the conversation going in that direction; so he tried to stick to the subject.

"You do know there are still a few downtown, don't you?" Sam paused long enough to swallow much of what was in his mouth, burped, then continued. "Hey, I know a good way to catch the slipperier morfs and spazzes who've managed to elude you even to this day. Here's what you do: Put on curly orange fright wigs and white pancake makeup and elevator shoes, and march down Derelict Hell Alley, and have some mean-assed drivers like yourself stationed in Black Marias at the other end of the street to scoop them up when they come scrambling out."

The driver shook his head, it seemed, in amazement at this barbarian's utter perspicacity—but it was hard to tell for sure

without seeing the bottom part of his face. He said, "That, or
something like it, was my assignment before the minister recruited
me."

Then the army men on the tanker truck began spewing
husky rice gruel into the beautiful gutters. Everybody forgot about
the unprecedented Red Flag and the hood ornament with the shiny
red toenails. They started to claw past one another and scramble
on their sable-black feet to fall face first in it: laundry, lavatory
and lunch collectivized.

Sam saw the real reason for the small girls' seating ar-
rangement. From their elevated position on the curb, they were
able more or less to gorge on the splashes from their elders' feed-
ing frenzy. Adoption of children is unpopular among the Red Chinese.

With one arm the driver dragged the whore back inside,
and the Red Flag passed out of Spaztown and into soggy commie
nighttime.

Tough Audience

How sharper than a serpent's tooth it is
To have a thankless child!
King Lear 1, 4, 281–289

Professor Edwine could hardly ever make his son laugh. From the time Sammy was a baby, the professor had tried to talk to him, had tested at least three dozen different anecdotes on his ears. It was essential to instruct this future chief of the Edwine tribe, to transmit clan lore, to be wise and close and chatty. But the kid hardly ever responded.

Eventually the professor got it refined down to a pair of tales about the olden days that at least held the boy's attention, and even got a slight smile out of him sometimes. It was necessary to tell these in a certain precise way to even get the kid to sit down. The professor fairly had to start talking in tongues, and had to get all physical and gesture a lot. He had to pay close attention to his phraseology and concinnities.

The first story was about the time when he was Sammy's age, and that old bloomer-button Tyrone Power came a-sashaying through the professor's hometown of Freeley, Idaho, on a hunting expedition. In the flesh, Tyrone Power, that handsome heartthrob. He wanted to be like old E. Hemingway because he was researching a part in a Hollywood version of one of Papa's books. Except nobody had been kind enough to tell the silly old thespian that there were no grizzlies or even antelope down this low on the western slope of the Teton Mountains. Tyrone had the cutest little leopard-skin jodhpurs on, all billowy and crinkly around his thighs.

(Here the old professor would prance a bit, knock-kneed, and Sam would watch impassively.)

"And, even though he was the rich bitch, everybody in the bar insisted on buying Ty-baby a drink. Banana daiquiri, if you puh-leeze? But Tyrone was unimpressed and bitchy-looking, like this.

(Here the old professor would pull the appropriate face, glad in his heart that no video camera was at hand, recording this moment to be smuggled into future family reunions.)

"And nobody wanted a big star like Tyrone Power to come away from Freeley with the impression that it was a boring place or anything like that. Oh, perish, Sammy! So they got me, old Easy Edwine, old string bean Edwine, all seven feet, one hundred and seventy pounds of me, clomp clomp, to do my famous trick, where I opened a bottle of beer with my bare teeth, held it straight up in the air with just my lips, no hands, Sammy, and let the whole twelve ounces pour straight down my gullet without swallowing.

(Here the professor would aim his face up at the ceiling and make gurgling sounds. Sammy might chuckle, just a tiny bit, if they were particularly good, gaggy-sounding gurgles, like Linda Lovelace being asphyxiated by a palomino.)

"'Lookit, Mr. Power!' the other Freeleyites yelled. 'Old Easy Edwine, he's a atheist bastard! He don't care!' And Tyrone was so intrigued that, as a climax, he had me break the bottle against my temple.

(Maybe cross-eyes and a cuckoo noise here.)

"Then Tyrone snuck out the back with his body guards and we were all alone, and so there was the nightly fight to the death, Sammy. And I woke up in a dry wash three miles outside of town next noontime, as per usual, with a four-inch gash on the side of my head, and the most elegant autograph on my Adam's apple. Tyrone had to stand on a barstool to reach it!"

The second tale of the olden days was about the time the carnival came to Freeley, Idaho. This was the same carny where Professor Edwine got the reach on the black pro-boxer and won the prize money. But that part had to be saved for his daughter, because his son didn't respond to stories like that, where Daddy was the protagonist instead of the comic relief.

And Sammy never wanted to hear the other heroic, self-complimentary carny tale, where Daddy was watering the elephants to earn his admission and this city woman was just standing in the midway, puffing a Kool in the shade of the tent flap and watching him work shirtless, obviously staring at him, up and down, a full twenty minutes, as he lugged those buckets, and Daddy knew he could have had her, right there on the spot. Old Jumbo could have sloppy seconds. That was a daughter-, not a son tale.

It was necessary to tell Sammy only the weird part of the carnival mythology, about the Pituitary Kid, the ten-foot-tall sideshow freako with a fifty dollar bill bobby-pinned to the crown of his head for anybody to keep who could reach it. Easy Edwine knelt among the crowd while the barker made the pitch, then stood up to his full height, and collected the dough simple as pie. He had to get up close to the Pituitary Kid's face, see his dead eyes, smell his sweet breath, feel the iron braces all up and down his rickety legs. The Pituitary Kid started crying softly and whispered, "Please, don't, Cousin. I'll lose my job. I'll become a ward of the state. Please back off, Cuz." And then the barker announced, through a giant yellow megaphone, to all of Freeley, that if they could bear to part with Easy Edwine, he was invited go on the road with the freak show!

That's where the professor sometimes got a response from his son: never any words, of course, but this slow, low grunting. It was communication, at least. Low-level, but communication. Sam would make the low sound until he got bored again, then just sort of wander away into another room, and the old professor would end feeling strange inside.

But you had to talk to your boy once in a while, no matter what. That was the rule. The only wisdom Professor Edwine still received from the Church of Jesus Christ of Latter-Day-Saints was their emphasis on the close-knit, communicative family.

The only other time Sammy would act interested in the lore of the olden days and in things pertaining to his father was when somebody brought out the crumbling copy of the September 6, 1939, Freeley Beacon and showed him the photo in the sports section of Freeley High School's new first string center. It was none other than Easy Edwine, his face mostly blank and full of question marks like it always was back in those days, wearing the too-small jersey destined to be retired with him, number double-zero, palming a basketball in each hand, arms out perpendicular in the crucified position, while two little forwards stood on tippy-toe underneath, one joker scowling upward into Easy Edwine's bony armpit and holding his nose.

The professor knew it was not for the right reasons that his son liked that yellowing old picture; but, surely, it imparted at least some sense of the Patriarchal past. And it got something not too unlike laughs out of the usually morose kid, a response.

So, on the day when Sammy said to his mother that certain too-familiar thing, that one extreme time when Sammy called his mom a fucking cunt and the professor disciplined him, smashed him up against the wall and choked him (the last time, probably, that anybody ever laid a hand on the kid in anger or affection or anything else), and Sammy's eyes went dead and he started that slow, low laugh of his, and his mother's fingernails were excavating the meat of the professor's big shoulder—that time, with Sammy laughing, it must have been almost by conditioned reflex, but the professor suddenly came up with another true story from the olden days he thought the kid might like, an actual WWII story, set in the Pacific Theater, where old Easy String Bean Edwine saw action and did his patriotic chore. And he told it in real high-falutin' style as he choked the life out of his only son's eyes.

"The short little Nips, Sammy, the way they run their POW camps makes the Bataan March look like a maypole dance. They starve your old dad's ass for months, keep it in a cage, tie it down to bamboo stakes, stomp on it, and then they get them a great big Nip, descended from sumos and samurais, Sammy, in peacetime a Nip sideshow attraction. And this freak meditates, rises up, screams his kamikaze-banzai scream and swings his sword down with all his fucking might to 'chop-choppee da big Amellican down to size.' Except the sumo-samurai guy knows a secret and profound oriental discipline, Sammy, and he can stop the blade short at just the split-second it just barely slices into the skin and tendons over your old dad's elongated shinbones. And he does it, night after night after night, his pals spitting and kicking, till they've got old string bean Edwine, your old dad, Sammy, laughing and screaming all the time. Even when he's asleep, even when he's chewing his weekly handful of rice husks."

The professor made a long, horrible wail right into his son's face, and they both started laughing. He let go of his son's throat in order to hold his sides. Sammy sank to the floor, gagging and coughing, and the professor hiked up his pants cuffs.

"See the scars, Sammy?"

And he was on the verge of finishing the story: escaping, shitting blood and rice and mucus nonstop in the jungle; and the last part he'd never told a single soul except his wife (only when he was half-asleep, cold sweating, up to his shins in nightmare), the last part showing what treatment like that can do to a guy's manhood.

But Sammy suddenly rolled over on his pudgy back and gasped, "Stop!"

There was a pause.

Sammy glanced over to his mother. The (quote) "fucking cunt" (close quote) had meanwhile sunk to the floor as well, flat on her nice butt, dead-eyed also, and bloody-fingernailed, making this certain "hup-hup hup" noise that meant it would soon be time to drop by the credit union for psych-ward money.

Sammy looked at his mother and listened to her. He used the knuckles of both fists to knead his windpipe more or less back open, and he sighed two times. Then, eyeing his mom as if for approval, he explained in a hoarse whisper why the professor should stop.

"Quit while you've got your audience rolling in the aisles, old Easy Edwine."

Sammy laughed, Ham-like, at his father's naked shins.

Catechumen

Suffering may well be called a baptism,
a regeneration, an initiation into a new state.
—George Eliot, Adam Bede

A baby strapped to either pair of shoulders, Polly and Mr. Fukuoka climbed up through a barely tended citrus grove to the summit of a tiny volcanic island. With each step their legs sank mid-calf deep into a mandarin orange-mulched loam that shimmered throughout with shattered fragments of black obsidian.

To the delight of the babies, hundreds of pink-eyed albino rabbits had been released, and millions of particolored wildflowers broadcast, Lady Bird Johnson-wise, in the first groping attempts of the Prefectural Ministry of Tourism to rehabilitate this notorious islet. The final demolition of its Rape of Nanjing-era poison gas factory was being blocked by some communists on the district council who wanted to make a grisly memorial of the place, second stop on the Hiroshima tourist's itinerary.

The factory ruins resembled a long-defunct Danish castle, except for the banana trees and wild poinsettias that sprouted from every crevice. The gray stone walls were covered with Ukiyoe-quality graffiti, the enormous ceramic vats filled knee-deep with discarded porno magazines. As they passed through the abandoned compound, Mr. Fukuoka tried to divert the children's attention away from the vats, toward the cliffs opposite and the countless minuscule crumbs of geology sprinkled into the middling vastness of the Seto Inland Sea.

Mr. Fukuoka had apparently saved up several weeks' worth of pocket change. Patiently, he'd waited for this rare sunny day, minus the nitrous oxides and hydrocarbon solids that normally palled the archipelago, making it look like Baghdad suffering a windless dawn. He'd arranged for a taxi to a remote dock, a tiny ferryboat, and a rental tandem bike which they could park at the base of the volcano. And, after going to all this expense and trouble, he'd wondered whether Polly and the babies would care to join him, no pressure to accept. He would show them a full-scale example of the reverse-perspective phenomenon observable in miniature on Japanese monochrome scrolls.

"Plus," he puffed, toeing the lip of the crater, "it's best to get the two akachan out in the sunlight from time to time, so they can absorb their vitamin D. They need extra amounts to help them metabolize the scanty nutrients in the local milk. Because of the mineral-poor volcanic soil in which the farmers must grow the grass they feed their cows, Japanese milk has only sixty percent of the calcium of American."

"Every mother expatriated here loses sleep over that," said Polly.

He warmed to the topic. "Did you ever notice how many children in this supposedly first-world country have black teeth?" It's far worse than China."

Polly had no reply to that.

Mr. Fukuoka shuffled his feet a bit, in apology for his last comment. As a catechumen at Hiroshima cathedral, a new candidate for baptism, he seemed to think it necessary to censor his impulses from time to time.

With averted eyes he said, "Perhaps you notice how I sometimes cringe when I am forced to say 'we' in reference to myself and the other children of the emperor. You see, I have spent much time in America. There are many who would say that fact alone makes me less Japanese—and they are more right than they can imagine."

Polly looked at him closely for the first time, to see if she could detect anything remotely American about him. There was something about the tight-buttocked way he carried himself, his narrow shoulders held as high as possible, almost in a shrug, as if to display an absent bosom, that made Polly wonder—but only idly, in passing, as she enjoyed her girls and the sunshine—about his sexuality.

Though his clothes were inexpensive and modestly styled, there was a certain fussiness in the way they were ironed and otherwise maintained. No buttons were missing, neither collar tip was curled up, and not a speck of any foreign substance was ground into the diagonal weave of this probable bachelor's twill pants.

Considering whose spouse she was, Polly was in no position to judge whether Mr. Fukuoka's fastidious grooming habits were compulsive or just normal. But he even fussed with the babies' clothes, and that struck her as definitely peculiar behavior for—she was forced to be gender-specific in this context—a man. He turned out both tiny collars to see whether, for whatever unimaginable reason, the girl's names had been magic-markered on the labels of garments that, with any luck at all, would be outgrown and passed on to pregnant neighbors in a matter of weeks.

"You know," he obviously and inexplicably lied, "it is an ancient tradition in this country for the father to mark the daughter's clothes. You should ask your husband to get a pen and—"

She must have looked at him oddly, for he immediately changed the subject.

"Now," he announced, "our reverse perspective phenomenon."

He gestured with a discreet thumb toward the neighboring peak. Polly shielded her eyes and peered across the threadlike strait separating this volcano from that. Sure enough, the inhabitants looked slightly larger than the oyster farmers toiling on the foothill beach of her own island.

Polly, with no binoculars at all, could make out a shantytown of chicken wire, scrap metal, clapboard and lath, rimming the extinct crater. Every hovel seemed to be draped with at least one war-surplus rising-sun banner, the old imperial style that embarrassed most modern Japanese so, with the scarlet radiations slithering out like invading armies to the frayed edges of the map.

This strange encampment was guarded by a regiment of combat-fatigued men of indeterminate age, their skulls shaven, their skins puckered from overexposure, if not to direct sunlight in this befouled archipelago, then at least to the more disease-ridden of its wavelengths. Smoking tiny bowled pewter pipes and tending their scale-model bonfires, they looked for all the world like the boy-sized, desiccated madmen who had dug into the Phillipine jungles and remained after the vaporization of this prefecture's capital city, worshiping and defending Hirohito for two generations after he stopped being God.

Several of them seemed to be fighting over whose turn it was to gawk at someone on this island through a pair of rusty old binoculars—evidently the reverse perspective business only worked one way.

"Those gentleman represent themselves as hunters," Mr. Fukuoka said, a sneer seeming almost ready to sprout on his face. "Their rifles are registered, one hundred percent legal, even though the biggest game around here, aside from the white rabbits, are these—"

He reached out at random and lifted a mandarin orange bough. Polly saw a half dozen of the fist-sized yellow and black spiders which drape their webs from any object in southern Japan that remains immobile for five minutes or more.

"They are the last straggling remnants of the so-called Youth Party," said Mr. Fukuoka. "They build their lives and personalities solely on resenting foreigners like you, Ms. Edwine, and your babies. But they won't bother us because they are cowardly. I'm afraid you will probably just have to content yourselves with jeers instead of bullets today."

But these racist troopers weren't even glancing at Polly. Even though she was conspicuously the foreigner, with saucer-sized eyes capable of flashing clear across the strait, and breasts displaying the salutary effects of a childhood nurtured on American dairy products, it was Mr. Fukuoka whom they found worthy of derision. Not just chapels full of Catholics, but craters full of fascists responded poorly to this man at first sight.

Some kind of unspoken attraction/revulsion was established between the two low peaks; and Polly's island-mate fell right into it, like a peg into the correct hole. He blushed, turning a shade of orange she'd never seen before, a satisfying hue which his brigade of tormentor seemed able to see plainly, for it only increased the volume of their cruel hoots.

Mr. Fukuoka responded to the Youth Party as readily as a damp-rimmed wineglass whines when rubbed by the rough ridges of a big man's fingerprint. He placed both fists on his narrow hips and stomped a girl-sized foot. Striking a petulant, jaw strutting pose, he tightened his buttocks and straightened his short spinal column even further.

He said, in a voice cracking like an aging diva's, "All young men are the same when they get into packs. Fortunately that particular pack is superstitious enough to keep off this island. It's the gas works that repel them."

He stepped into a beam of sunlight and waved his arm down the slope at the ruins, calling the neighbor's attention to the giant mustard vats. And several of them did seem to shrink a bit, to retreat for succor into their huts.

"See?" said Mr. Fukuoka, his voice returning as he gained the upper hand over the enemy. "There were several accidents during the war, and hundreds of schoolgirls, conscripted to stir the phosgene, died horribly. The military officials kept the details secret to avoid insurrections among the local fisherman, who had controlled this whole arm of the sea as privateers not that long before. It's said that many unmarked bone yards are concealed under these orange trees, and until the records are unearthed, the guilt acknowledged, and the girls' remains identified and given proper cremations, this place cannot be consecrated for worship. It is the one island, unique among the eight hundred-plus in this entire godforsaken country, that has no religious structure. In the meantime, it's as unlucky as a volcano can be, short of outright eruption. So we are safe from the stalwart patriots next door."

As he spoke, his voice and eyes exuded scorn for Japan. This was unprecedented in any Nihonjin of Polly's acquaintance. Embarrassment she'd seen, even shame. Sadness and regret, certainly, and hatred as well. But never had she encountered contempt for his or her homeland in a Japanese.

"You lived in America?" she asked.

But the wince of the entire left side of his body indicated regret that he'd mentioned that place, and a deep reluctance to discuss it further. Not surprisingly, he'd allowed himself to have bad times there.

How bad had his times been here?

Polly realized that she'd been assuming, in the back of her guilt-ridden American mind, that this sad little man was not only a native of Hiroshima City, but a hibakusha—one of those who'd been within a kilometer of the epicenter, who must, twice yearly, for the rest of their lives, report to the Radiation Effects Research Foundation on top of Mount Hijiyama for agonizing liver biopsies. She hadn't studied enough of the local dialect to be able to identify Mr. Fukuoka's origins strictly from his speech.

As if he'd read her mind, he waved his arm into the blue distances and said, "Nobody heard a thing except for a couple of fisherman out there." He pointed to a broad quadrant of sea water at their feet, its greasy surface writhing, pleasure-launches and tuna boats bobbing, over the indigo maneuvers of a Self-Defense-Forces submarine, silent and bat like.

"I wonder if you could see the mushroom from this spot," said Polly, watching his face, learning nothing.

"I'm sure you could. The boilers in the, ah, munitions fac-tory wouldn't have been stoked that early in the morning."

He began to stare so unblinkingly long and hard at the babies that Polly wondered if he'd had a sudden stroke or some-thing. She wanted to see if it was still possible to get his attention, but shrank from touching his shoulder.

She thought it might be a good idea to say his first name loudly and firmly into his ear, but she didn't know it. So she decided on a kind of compromise.

"If it's not too personal a question, Fukuoka-san," she al-most shouted, "I'm curious as to what you've chosen to be chris-tened."

He broke his baby-gaze long enough to glance self-consciously at her. He murmured, "Philip."

"Oh? After Saint Philip Neri?"

"Philip the Deacon. Protector of orphans."

He selected a baby to lift onto his shoulders, piggyback style. But first he primly sniffed for a soiled diaper. This brought a resumption of jeers from the crater next door, accompanied by a couple of flashes of light and puffs of smoke.

Substitutes

"Because of our ancient Confucian traditions, we Chinese don't find any bad connotations in the name Big Brother."

The student who spoke had something downtrodden and emaciated about him that was alien to his classmates, and to Polly, the substitute teacher, as well. The extreme slit-eyes set at almost forty-five-degree angles to the mouth full of buck teeth, several of which needed western-style root canals; the way he insisted on hunkering on the window sill during break time like a cruel nineteenth-century newspaper caricature of a celestial: this was the white supremacist's quintessential Chinaman. The only thing missing was the plaited queue, and Polly had difficulty not imagining it behind the tiny sunburnt head, tucked under the unfashionable blue collar.

The other students found him unacceptable, and now were laughing at him. He pretended to ignore them and stood, reverting to the formal Chinese classroom etiquette which Polly's husband, Sammy, had demolished long ago. He was taking urgent exception to the sobriquet of the dictator in the novel they'd finished and laid to rest half a semester earlier.

"For us Big Brother is something fine, a bastion of society. We Chinese look to our elder brother in moments of dire anguish. We respect him and he, in turn, treats us kindly, and—"

The crueler, bolder boys (Polly sometimes caught herself thinking of them as boys, though they were thirty and fathers, many of them) began, in loud voices, to say mean things in their native idiom, forgetting, or refusing to believe, that Polly could understand. Two years of homilies in the underground church, accompanied by Gregorian chant transliterated from the Vulgate into the local street lingo, had given her a rough proficiency. She and Sammy were the first foreigners to have learned the dialect since the communists threw the missionaries out.

From the back of the room came scoffing voices.

"Yes, that may be. But Xiao Bu's elder brother can't be looked to in this particular moment of dire anguish. At least not from this vantage point. He's fifteen years down the turd-hole of history and still hasn't managed to graduate from the rustication program."

"Don't be uncharitable. It's not that he failed to graduate. It's just that he wishes to remain in the countryside to serve the people."

There were giggles from the girls, rather, the women, who arranged themselves in the front row every day, as infatuated with Polly as American sixth-graders with their new gym teacher. They were delighted that Sammy had long ago abdicated in favor of her. It was these women who had rendered her name Po Li, Active and Lovely. They always gathered around her on break-time, under the jealous scrutiny of the young man at whom they laughed now, and talked about her big dark eyes.

"You could be Chinese," they'd say, paying her the highest compliment imaginable, followed by the inevitable "So why don't you have children?"

Then, when the bell rang, they'd rearrange themselves immodestly in the tiny missionary-style school benches, each draping at least one of her legs over somebody else's, so that many pairs of underpants showed. Their thighs were fat-free and tended to be extremely white, for, as urban Chinese, these women avoided sunshine. The lovely tans of which they were capable were considered declasse. This probably had as much as anything to do with their giggling at the idea of serving the peasants.

The semi-conscious underpants display was the main reason Sammy had hung on as long as he had. He called it "the leg show" and found in it endless fascinations both wholesome and unwholesome. "Their level of repression is so deep that they've lost any conception of the privacy of their own genitalia," he marveled. "Collectivized crotch, I call it."

At any moment Polly expected uniformed men to bang down the door in search of her husband, to arrest him for whatever he'd been doing at night lately rather than sleeping in their fruitless bed. She took solace in one thought: if they came, the authorities would not find Sammy here, for he no longer came any closer to the classroom buildings than to their squalid room in the barbarian compound.

He had started a model teacher, to his own and Polly's amazement. Teacher San Mu, the walking encyclopedia, the students had called him, and invited him to the bookless reading room to talk. During the first semester everybody, Sammy as well as the students, had done beautifully on 1984—so beautifully, in fact, that sometimes Polly found herself shifting nervously in the special observer's seat reserved for provincial cadres who never showed up. (Even in those distant halcyon days she'd had premonitions of educational doom, and had hoped her presence might delay their coming true.)

Under Orwell and Sammy's subversive influence, dangerous things had been said out loud, right in class: a non-revisionist history of the party is impossible to get in China, but in Hong Kong and America books as true as Emanuel Goldstein's are openly distributed; the insidious processes of Newspeak can be recognized in Mao's attempts to "de-feudalize" Chinese characters—a whole catalog of such oral braveries. Polly would kick her husband and make discreet warning nods in the direction of the party informant (his head always down, seeing nothing, hearing everything, taking copious notes in the back of the grimy classroom); but Sammy and the students would laugh and proclaim with one voice, "Animals and English majors are free!"

In the halls, in the dorms, in the nightmarish rest rooms, big-character posters suddenly appeared in English, Chinese, Japanese, even Russian:

WAR IS PEACE

FREEDOM IS SLAVERY

IGNORANCE IS STRENGTH

Sammy knew exactly who'd painted and posted these incendiary da zhi bao, and he was delighted to be taken into the confidence of such stout comrades. He said he felt just like one of the boys. Being a male Anglo Saxon from a prosperous far-western community, he'd never had much experience with this sort of thing. He was still in high school when the draft ended, and only got in on one anti-Nixon rally. His personal contact with police officers was limited to the night he got stuck somewhere in the sagebrush outside Provo and a highway patrolman gave him a canful of unleaded and five dollars. So thumbing his nose at totalitarianism—or at least inciting his pupils to thumb theirs—was a new and exciting experience for Polly's plighted spouse.

For the first time he began to see a connection between life and livelihood. "I had to come to a Marxist/Leninist society to learn the importance of job identity," he said. He would wake up at night mumbling that his heart felt like it was expanding down there among his ribs, and set to work on new lecture notes under the mosquito net.

One day the pregnant pinto cat from the cafeteria was no longer pregnant, but no kittens were in sight—just four particularly smug and plump rats lounging in a damp patch of earth out back, a classic Daoist omen. The students' expository essays began mysteriously to de-politicize and sink to innocuous topics like child-rearing, and to be accepted for publication by the op-ed folks at China Daily, where they'd formerly been rejected with indignation.

Then the class switched, as the syllabus had given ample warning it would, from Twentieth-Century Dystopias to Contemporary American Novels in Verse (a bibliographically manageable area of study, Sammy assured them); and their pirated mimeographs of the equally verboten Pale Fire turned out blurry, and the class lost its aim, flopped. No voices but the teacher's drone were heard any longer. The "party suck," as Sammy would've referred to him, felt the time ripe to move to the front of the class.

Sammy's complaints about living conditions and bureaucracy and "giraffe-in-the-zoo syndrome" began at about this time. Polly was sure these now-perpetual laments were just a way of camouflaging his shock at discovering a spy in his classroom. Intellectually, of course, it was no surprise and was even amusing to him; but emotionally it was a kick in the face that left a bruise he could never acknowledge to himself or Polly. It would have made him seem naive, an apple-pie-and-milk American boy come bang against political reality for the first time at the age of thirty-plus.

In self-defense, Polly's husband had developed a rotten attitude toward his professional responsibilities and toward China in general. She should've foreseen this. Ever since the afternoon of their wedding, when he'd collared a ripe, uninvited transient at the communion rail and grilled him on transubstantiation (a "doctrinal issue" he'd cited, along with his gout, to excuse his own non-participation in the Eucharist), Sammy had been reacting against what he considered Polly's liberal guilt-inspired politeness. And now he set out singlehandedly to demolish the myth of the American "foreign experts" as youngish Peace Corps types trying to assimilate themselves gently into Asia.

He shouted down wrong numbers with the ugliest gibberish that could be squeezed between clenched teeth. He stepped with all his might on toes in the street, well aware of the calcium deficiency endemic among these frail people. He gave not a centimeter in the bike lanes, using his triple mass and momentum to send other cyclists sprawling, and flagrantly violated the law by not stopping at the scene of the accident to "work out contradictions" for an hour of fleeting Chinese time. In shops, even state-run ones, he dickered in vicious dialect for twenty minutes at a time, then let the few coppers he'd bled from the shopkeepers slip from his wallet. The very merchants he'd just bullied, having lost the screaming match only because the shock of an enormous waiguoren howling within arm's length was so distracting, would be obliged to chase his enormous strides down the street or risk being imprisoned for damaging their country's reputation for honesty in petty things. He was out of control more and more lately.

Sometimes he'd wake her up in the middle of the night and ask her something like, "How the fuck do you maintain such an attitude among these commies?"

And she'd begin to explain to him that she believed in Heaven and Hell, had tried many times to imagine them both, and that Hell had nothing to do with physical discomfort nor even political oppression, but consisted of the total absence of God, and that no place on earth could ever be unbearable to someone who had faith in God's immanence as well as transcendence, and that such faith could be based on a general intuition, the kind Sammy said he felt at certain moments with music or novels, or even with her sometimes, and he'd be snoring before she could finish.

Something vestigially Puritan in Sammy had made him spend part of one early afternoon finding a justification for putting his wife to work while he wandered the streets on his bicycle searching for immanence among the open sewers. He decided that all (instead of just most) of the students were secretly hoping to be assigned jobs as interpreters for China Travel Service when they graduated so they could get rich on bribes from the foreign-class hotels; and that, short of flunking (which would be disastrous) they were deliberately trying not to distinguish themselves academically because the university tended to fasten onto the best students and doom them to a life of professorial poverty. And a knowledge of Contemporary American Novels in Verse was not exactly essential to the future tour guides of the Middle Kingdom, who weren't even expected to be familiar with their own culture before the Beginning of Everything in 1949.

But the shreds of the Orwellian big-character posters still flapped from some of the walls; and it had been, Polly now realized, mainly to win back the affection of his students that Sammy had resorted to his grand finale of pedagogical hooliganism: over Polly's near-hysterical objections he had distributed copies of a sabotage and assassination manual which he thought they'd appreciate, a souvenir from his high school days and what he called the "summer of extreme boredom."

"Remember," he'd said while walking out the door for the last time, "ignition systems are basically the same in all modern automobiles, even those driven by your unelected leadership."

"Several chuckled, didn't they?" he'd beamed when she came home from finishing the rest of the class period. "They almost acknowledged my presence in Asia today, huh?"

Polly had at that moment decided to bestir herself from the passive observer's seat and to upgrade her academic status to teacher's aide before he got them both deported or cremated or something. Like a dutiful wife, she found herself expending most of her psychic energy pondering the preservation of Hubby's career (such as it was). She only hoped his hide wouldn't need preserving soon.

Polly had taken over the postgraduate English and American literature course with the blessings of Cao Xiwei, the Samuel Johnson-quoting dean of the foreign languages department. Professor Cao somehow figured that, since Sammy was a white foreigner, anybody who got into his good graces would automatically be invited to the British Isles on a visiting lectureship that would blossom into an immigration permit and a romantic, affluent means of jettisoning wife and children. He called Polly an "occidental beauty," and every time they passed in the halls reminded her of the amazement he felt whenever the students turned in glowing reports of her teaching skills.

"So lovely and yet so active," Professor Cao would marvel in his perfect Oxford accent; and, when Polly brought up some administrative problem long neglected by Sammy, this tweedy little Chinese would look very carefully at his watch—it always required inordinate effort for him to ascertain the hour, for he kept it set to Greenwich mean time—and he would say, "Oh, sorry Dear, but I must be popping off."

She'd been foolish to worry that a man like that would trouble himself over the formal qualifications of the teachers in his charge. She wished she hadn't hesitated to assume the podium on Professor Cao Xiwei's account; for she worried now that, before bestirring herself, she had allowed Sammy to do some serious damage to the poor young man standing before the class today, this Big Brother-obsessed Xiao Bu.

It was hardly surprising, here in this nephewless, nieceless place ten thousand miles from home, that her doomed maternal instincts should find an outlet in this boy. There she went again, referring to men her husband's age as boys.

But then, maybe she knew at least one "boy" who wasn't Chinese at all.

Sammy, even more than the others, seemed to hate Xiao Bu. His every action toward him was a scream: "I know it was you who betrayed your classmates and spoiled our momentum in the dystopia unit!" Time and again Polly tried to tell her husband that he'd mixed Xiao Bu up with the real informant, that Xiao Bu wasn't the only party member in class; but Sammy refused to listen, sputtering something self-consciously racist about them all looking alike. Polly hoped this indignation, though misplaced, was genuine, and that Sammy hadn't alighted upon Xiao Bu just because of his craven and subjugated personal appearance, the defenseless look of the natural-born victim.

One good thing had come of Sammy's absenting himself, besides the possible foiling of policemen who might come around hungry for his blood: he seemed to have taken the real "party suck" with him.

Perhaps the informant had been given orders to suspend his book learning in order to perform fieldwork, a kind of on-the-job totalitarian-tool training, by following Sammy around. Polly had to admit that slogging after Sammy through the mud streets of this city would be better preparation for the future of that particular boy than slogging after Vladimir Nabokov through the pages of his most difficult non-novel. In any case, the faithful informant was conspicuous in his absence today.

Polly could not imagine why her otherwise fairly intelligent husband had mixed Xiao Bu up with the real Iscariot among his disciples. The spy (whose name Polly could never remember) was almost a Hollywood-B stereotype of treachery personified: smooth and compliant in all small things. Xiao Bu, on the other hand, had all the smoothness of a Heilongjiang street with frost-heave, and displayed open moral indignation at Sammy and his syllabus—when Sammy wasn't around, of course. And, if he'd been compliant enough on several occasions to allow Sammy to borrow his considerable linguistic skills to extract himself from various snake pits of bureaucracy, it had only been an impersonal favor— "one's duty," as Xiao Bu put it.

"This is the south," Sammy would jeer in front of everybody after accepting Xiao Bu's help. "A man of gumption gets ahead outside the party here, by exhibiting the entrepreneurial virtues. You belong in Manchuria, Mosquito Lunch, in Mukden among the moldering Maoists."

And when the poor boy was chagrined to the point of hesitating to come down from his hunker on the window sill, Sammy would threaten to report him for insubordination—a threat that under normal Chinese circumstances would have been ineffective. Everybody knew that barbarians' opinions on classroom comportment were less than meaningless. Administrators were expected to heed only the reports of the party informant and the classroom monitor. And, as far as Sammy knew, they were one and the same person in this case: Xiao Bu himself.

But there was something lupine and sociopathic about the way this big-nosed outlander mouthed the word insubordination that compelled Xiao Bu to come down and be seated among his snickering classmates, even though the only seats left were in the front row next to females.

"Oooh! Mosquito Lunch has a girlfriend!" Sammy would squeal, just to get a few chuckles. Polly suspected the chuckles were not aimed at the person Sammy had intended them for. But, as he said, it was good for killing a few seconds of class time.

"The teacher is a professional ass-maker," he was fond of revealing. "And as long as he has the opportunity to practice his craft, it matters little whom he practices it on, himself or his students."

And here stood Xiao Bu now, Sammy's latest product, alone as anyone could be in a stuffed Chinese classroom, shunned by all, convinced deep in his soul that Polly's husband hadn't abdicated his grading rights just yet, and that he, Mosquito Lunch, was about to be flunked on general principles and exiled degreeless to some bleak office in a village even remoter than the one his ostensible elder brother was mired in.

Polly's heart went out to him. It would be impossible for a foreigner, especially a brash American, to imagine the extent of the boy's anguish. Public ridicule was not practiced in this country except under the most violent circumstances. Sammy should've known that.

Polly understood now that it was for Xiao Bu's sake that she had agreed to take over and let Sammy spend his time hanging out at his favorite fancy hotel on the south side of town. She hoped her husband's new off-campus friends, whoever they were, would teach him a little compassion. For Sammy was a textbook sadist in many ways, a masochist as well.

As part of the formal procedures for removing him from the classroom, Sammy's graduate committee back in the States had addressed a formal communique to the Dean of Humanities. The document indicated that they had detected "little evidence of the nurturing instinct in this particular teaching-fellow."

Of course, the self-destroyer inside Sammy had provided photocopies of this communique to anybody in China interested enough to look, and had passed around the name and address of a certain mail order house specializing in fake diplomas—once he'd gotten here on the free flight, that is.

He'd only just gotten his own wife on that plane, accessory to fraud, with a "whither thou goest" that convinced her not by Biblical precedent, but by the searing self-hatred in the voice he'd used to quote the Book of Ruth. She'd come along not only to protect the Xiao Bu's of China from him, but him from himself.

What kind of father would such a man have made? A moot question now. No, not just now. It had been for thirty-plus years. It was only Polly who had recently found out it was moot. Maybe that's why God allowed Sammy to be the way he was, inclined to cruelty towards creatures under his domination and in his charge, creatures unable to respond in kind: for none were fated to be there for the first quarter of a life, only for quarters of years.

But was it really sadism, or just audience awareness? People laughed so easily at Xiao Bu, and it was impossible for a man of her husband's temperament to pass up a laugh, with all its implicit popular approval, however fleeting—especially in enemy territory, which is what Sammy considered any classroom to be.

On those monthly occasions when, just by routine, with no justification that they were aware of (for the goings-on in the classroom meant nothing to them), the foreign affairs department refused to give Sammy his money, or withheld the scrip for his kidney-stone anesthetics, Xiao Bu was there to help with the screaming and the desk-pounding.

Polly's dialect was passable, but her Mandarin was ludicrous; and the foreign affairs department was ruled by old Mandarin-belching militarists and hard-line Maoists from up north, whom Deng Xiaoping considered too unsocialized to be presentable anywhere near the centers of national policy-making, where a significant foreigner might catch a whiff of them. Everybody but tiny, silly-looking Xiao Bu was terrified even to approach the armed guard at the administration compound gate; and Xiao Bu was ready to put his party membership in jeopardy by helping a foreigner's wife (doubly low) to storm the payroll office.

"Your husband was invited to our country by the National Ministry of Education, and he is on a standard contract that must be honored by both parties," said Xiao Bu without a trace of irony in his voice. "If Dr. Edwine doesn't get paid, he will be unable to leave China. (He was planning to leave eventually, wasn't he?) Our leaders must be made to understand that the law is on his side. It's only a matter of getting past a few corrupt clerks at the lower levels of the bureaucracy. It is these small potatoes, and not the ling dao, who are the 'red bandits' Chiang Kai Shek had so much to say about—but please don't quote me, Teacher Po Li, if you love your little Xiao Bu."

And he soon learned where such idealism would get him when the ravenous lesbian department chief smashed him against the wall, in full view of Polly, and screamed in his ear, "You can't bring big-noses in here! This is the foreign affairs department! What's your name and unit number?"

Xiao Bu had to write self-criticisms for a month, for he had shattered the cardinal principal upon which this society, both dynastic and post-dynastic, had been based: he had tried to talk to a superior more than three tiers higher than himself.

According to the bona-fide American professors who came to China on plush short-term sabbaticals, this elitist corruption was part of the realistic charm of the Middle Kingdom, like the rats and the forty-percent hepatitis rate. But even they were shocked to hear of this southern foreign affairs department behaving like the shameless, "faceless" felons at a northern sham institution such as, for example, the notorious Beijing University.

Xiao Bu's studies in the 1984 unit had to slide a bit while he performed the auto-brainwashing of self-criticism, and Sammy, of course, feigned outrage. He offered to flunk the boy, and was never persuaded to believe the tale of the siege of the payroll office. He had been at a banquet at the time with some extracurricular friends. But that didn't stop him from using it as a source of new mockery.

"So, Mosquito Lunch fancies himself a servant of the people, does he?" Sammy cried, loud enough for everyone to hear, giving a mock Young Pioneers salute and swilling Snowflake beer purchased with renminbi that the boy had just procured for him.

Polly now called on Xiao Bu to answer the question she'd secretly coached him on beforehand, so he could shine forth in class and salvage some of the face that her husband had so systematically eroded from his prominent cheekbones. Xiao Bu was by far the brightest, but required extra help because he preferred reading books off the reading list, older ones, like *A Tale of Two Cities*, from the era before Freud (whom he considered a bourgeois reactionary). "Your husband teaches only counterrevolutionary pornography," Xiao Bu complained, though he assumed he'd better master it for his future's sake.

Just as she'd coached him (he was too straightforward to have thought of it himself) he paused to give the other students a fair chance to answer the question themselves—which they never did.

The silence of the unresurrected tomb fell over the rows of drooping black heads. It was possible to hear the amazing rats that brawled in the room across the dark corridor: hell room, where the garbage of the three years' existence of this already decaying building had been swept and retained for unimaginable reasons. The creatures thrashed among the liquefying refuse, making noises like the hundredth-generation Nile crocodiles in their open sewer at the zoo.

Under this distressing layer of sound she could hear the idle clerks behind their locked departmental office door screaming over a cramped ping-pong game, rules and walls modified to resemble those of racquetball. Their bare feet sloshed among the defrosting yellow croakers, rejects from Sammy's banquet hotel. It was payday, and the Edwines weren't the only people around here expected to live without cash. The renminbi substitutes were aging more rapidly than they should have in this late-February lunar new year's weather, because the clerks—three thin-blooded oldish ladies—had been mistakenly given an extra ration of coal for their foot-warming stove and refused to bank the flames even after their enclave grew hot, ostensibly because they didn't want to blacken their fingers for fear of smudging the non-existent official paperwork they had no intention of touching in this anarchist's dream-university.

Polly knew they had, by this time, stripped to their old Chinese ladies'-style underwear, the cotton short-shorts and the tank-topped tee shirts over tiny unbrassiered breasts that, after fifty, began to sag just enough to resemble youngish western breasts.

They loved Polly dearly. She was the only person they allowed into the office. (Even Dean Cao Xiwei had never gotten much more than his nose past the door.) They dragged her in almost every day to coo over her curly hair and attempt to commiserate with her for having such a rhino for a husband.

"How do you know about rhinos?" Polly had asked once, condescending without meaning to.

"We saw your man every day for almost a whole month, and you ask us how we know about rhinos?"

Now their strange shrieks mixed with the miasma of the faculty toilet down the hall, which, Xiao Bu assured her, in desperately apologetic tones, was shocking even by southern Chinese standards.

When she had her period and had to make visits to that pit of uncirculated sewage, Polly had to force herself to recall the gist of her midnight homilies to her snoring husband on the subject of the impossibility of hell on earth. At that time of month, only one thing saved her from playing truant like Sammy before her (aside from the knowledge that they were on work visas and too broke to shift to tourist visas, and one of them had to look occupied to keep them both from being deported to a place where Sammy was unemployable). It was that one solid fact about herself that she'd always known, something as essential to her personality as her religion. Though she'd abandoned her own teaching opportunities to follow Sammy here, she was a teacher.

And here were students. Despite their age, cultural circumstances had conspired to make the members of this class resemble empty vessels ranged before her.

They were taking the opportunity of the real spy's absence today to indulge in some free-ish speech a la the pre-crackdown Sammy days. Their dialect jeering at Xiao Bu began to assume a somewhat political dimension, as the question of his being class monitor was broached.

"Nobody else could be persuaded to take the job."

"Yes, the rest of us have things to do outside this classroom, such as live life."

Xiao Bu tilted back his head and began to recite a poem in the classical style by Mao, which Polly only caught the gist of: something about there being no life outside the collective, and this being obvious to anybody who has boned up on his Marx and Lenin, etc.

As could be expected, the others laughed at the mere mention of Marx, Lenin, even—maybe especially—Mao. They were apolitical from apathy as well as blissful ignorance. The ideological excesses of the Ten Years' Chaos would never be repeated among these people.

And yet, when pressed to make some kind of critical appraisal of a literary work—and they had to be reminded in the strongest terms that critical appraisals were a major part of the course requirements, regardless of the one-man-circus her husband had mounted in the terminal stages of his tenure—none of them turned out to have anything but the stale Marxist clichés in his/her mind:

Ginsberg, the personification of Death in Malamud's short story, should be regarded with the utmost respect because, as a tickettaker in a railroad station, he is serving the people. Dreiser and Jack London are America's two greatest writers. Rip Van Winkle is a tragic and not a comic figure because he slept through his country's glorious revolution.

"Not unlike certain of our classmates' big brothers."

"Oh, but Elder Mosquito Lunch took an active role in his country's latest revolution. It's just modernization he's slept through."

And when, outside the critical mode, they mocked Marx and their own party cell secretary, they displayed a pure cultural nihilism. Nothing else but animal greed was there to fill the ethical void.

The place was a physical hell, and the students were frolicking without joy on the rim of a moral purgatory. Polly had been cast in the role of Virgil for now, and hoped auditions for Beatrice were still open. She wouldn't leave these children until somebody deported her.

"Teacher Po Li, I don't know about Nabokov's positive, but I do think that Orwell has one," Xiao Bu was saying, ignoring Polly's coaching to return to the previous unit's book. His earnest need to express whatever he was about to say had overcome his desire to shine in class.

"That positive, paradoxically, is a fascist and sadist. In the act of writing the book, Orwell discovered a devil-god inside himself, infinitely wise, infinitely cynical, named O'Brien, capable of the most treacherous crimes. Including murder."

His small voice rose with such blackened passion on the last word that even the girls stopped giggling for a brief moment, then resumed twice as loud as before.

Princessing Lessons

My solitude grew more and more obese, like a pig.
—Mishima Yukio

Not too long ago, a young career diplomat named Owada was purchased to grace the bedchamber of Emperor Hirohito's princely grandson.

She was sold by her grandfather, who just happened to be a big wheel in the chemical company that poisoned all those Japanese fishermen with mercury back in the '60s. The court case, which dragged on for several decades, was miraculously settled in her grandpa's favor the day after Owada agreed to pour her robust blood into the inbred royal family's languishing gene pool.

In the days when she was still merely the future Crown Princess of Japan, Owada was compelled to kneel down and submit to certain attentions from the Head Chamberlain of the Board of Ceremonies. Within the confines of the Imperial Court this was known as "re-education." Unfortunately, the curriculum this strange old man had been authorized to impart, and the syllabus he had laid out, were not exactly designed to transfix the attention of a woman schooled at Oxford and Harvard.

Her engagement to the Crown Prince hadn't yet been leaked to the press at that time, but Owada was expected to hunker on a rice-straw mat for several hours each day while this ninety-four-year-old former classmate of Hirohito ranted into the close air between their faces. Fortified with powdered rhinoceros horn and benzedrine-spiked "health drinks," he liked to drum calligraphy brushes on the low-slung lacquered table in the Main Hall of the Togu palace.

Upon considering him for the first time, she'd noticed that his femurs and tibias were peculiarly elongated, as if the law of gravity had been repealed in his vicinity, and that his skin was hairless as a Japanese woman's, his voice squeaky. But he'd read her thoughts before she herself had time to fashion them from unconscious impulse.

Prefacing his introductory lecture with a demure glance down at his own indigo-draped lap, he'd said, "The Japanese court never fell into that most dangerous trap: We never maintained a class of eunuchs. And why is this? Well, young lady, as I will try again and again to impress upon your consciousness, we inhabitants of these chambers are all members of a single and unique tribe, the true Yamato people, the great- great- great- great- (et cetera – no need to belabor the point) grandsons and -daughters of Amaterasu the Sun Goddess. And one simply does not emasculate one's brothers and sisters."

Quickly catching himself in his own absurdity, he switched to a language he considered more appropriate for giggling, and added, "Surtout pas des soeurs!"

He called a brief halt in whatever brainless drill they happened to be engaged in — the ikebana, the waka, the anal-retentive penmanship, the lexicon of rarefied pronouns she had to master before speaking or being spoken to as Princess — and he dismissed the retainers from the Main Hall for a couple of minutes (thus guaranteeing their eavesdropping on the other side of the paper door).

Clearing his throat, he declared, "Numinosity, the supernatural sublime, is all. That's why you mustn't fret, my dear, when we take the better part of the night and the day to deck you out in your wedding dress."

Stretching out a bony, hairless hand and clamping onto her wrist, the ancient courtier let Owada know in no uncertain terms that suiting up was infinitely the most important part of her re-education. The very soul and essence of her existence from now on would be the clothes she was to wear at the hyper-secret court ceremonies, of which her wedding was but the least arcane.

"I've heard your mother complain in the broadcast media

that she could never get you into traditional garb as a child. Nevertheless, you did eventually master the difficult art of donning kimono, did you not?"

"Yes," lied Owada.

"Excellent. Wonderful. Now forget everything you ever learned. On lofty occasions you'll be wearing Heian-style clothing, which requires several hours longer to put on, with you standing motionless on a special wooden turntable most of that while. The Heian period is pre-kimono — I assume you assimilated that much during what little schooling you received in our empire between bouts of globe-trotting."

He almost swished himself flat onto his back.

"The twelve-tier bridal gown allows you artfully to show your under layers, in all the subtle varieties of shade and pattern. The Heian authors could gush on for hundreds of pages, rhapsodizing over this style. Clothes were even a medium of exchange back then. You allowed your left wrist to dangle coyly from the window of the Imperial palanquin in the afternoon, and by evening the entire eastern end of the Silk Road was positively convulsed!"

He left her to ponder that sobering thought until deep in the night, when the unconscious is spread wide open and receptive in all but the most unhappy, displaced insomniac. Then, under cover of wee-hour blackness, he materialized in the princely bridegroom's bed chamber, a bit blurry around the edges, and smug as a ghost to whom had been granted, by Imperial fiat, the right to slide open the beige paper door without having all four of his extenuated limbs fractured by the retired police matron who stationed herself in the corridor throughout the night.

It was the first of the prescribed three nights preceding the nuptials, when "bridal breach" was supposed to be effected by the prince on a rice-straw floor mat, according to ancient and esoteric Yamato tradition. At the key moment (and to the bride's eternal gratitude), Prince Naruhito had clambered to his minuscule feet and vanished as sheepishly as the Son of Heaven can vanish. And when the door slid back open, it was not a flaccid husband who stood there in the shadows, but the cagey pseudo-eunuch himself, decked out in a kimono of deepest indigo and matching slippers, come to provide his catechumen with yet more Shintoist wisdom.

He squatted, or perhaps fell, on crackling knees and shoved his face right down next to hers. Heavy purple European wine laced his breath.

"Tell me, girl," he croaked. "Who is the happiest person you know?"

Owada covered her nipples with the fringe of Prince Naruhito's silken futon. "I don't understand the question," she said.

"Come now. How easy can a question be? Who is it?"

She widened her eyes and waited. Eventually the old man flitted one eye toward the shoji door.

Even if her heavy breath hadn't been seeping through the paper panel, it would've been a safe bet that Owada's babysitter / bodyguard hulked out there. Did that mammoth creature stand till dawn? Owada had never seen a chair anywhere up or down the length of the gloomy hall.

From the very first coy whispers of a princely pulse quickening, Owada's babysitter / bodyguard had manned her post faithfully as a Saint Bernard. The woman was a given in Imperial life, yet she filled a position that had by no means developed into a tradition, therefore received no mention in this seminar on tradition. Hers was the sole presence in the palace for which the Head Chamberlain offered no explanation and n no gossip. Owada had never been provided with a proper means of referring to her. Somehow, "my babysitter / bodyguard" seemed a tad impertinent, so Owada said nothing. For a full minute they listened to the woman's labored breath.

As if some major point had been made, the Head Chamberlain sprang back to his feet with strange effortlessness, and began to pace back and forth in the tiny space available to him. In a whistling wheeze that seemed to emanate feebly from the shallower lobes of his humid lungs, he addressed the next Empress of Japan, naked and perfumed in her unconsummated bridal bed. He told her revised versions of stories she'd heard at bedtime all her life.

"Offended by her younger brother's spreading his feces all over her nice private things, torturing dumb animals, and waving his genitalia in her face — all those sorts of naughty, masturbatory, infantile high jinks which have been the hallmark of Japanese maleness ever since – Amaterasu the Sun Goddess retired to a cave, something like I imagine your cold dorms of Oxford to have been. She deprived the outside world of her sunshine presence, plunging all into darkness and chaos, only to be distracted from her self-pity by the feigned, and more than a little lewd, merry-making of her fellow divinities: giggling strip teases and so on. The divine whore, Uzume, was recruited to make the goddess crack a smile, and to bring light back to the world by luring her out, utilizing a mirror to bounce her smile abroad.

"And Amaterasu was given this magical mirror as a souvenir of her own petulance. To this day it is preserved as one of the Royal Regalia, along with the sacred sword which her little brother plucked from the Hell-Serpent's tail, only to surrender it immediately to her in a gesture of abject apology and eternal self-subjugation."

The Head Chamberlain segued to a Frenchy English and said, "Remember, mon cheri, that also counted among the Royal Regalia are the Most Auspicious Curved Jewels. These shapely gems were presented to the Imperial Progenetrix directly from the hands of the Celestial Deities in the dim days before history began. That places the Empress — and this means you, eventually — in a position unique in the cosmos. Make no mistake about it."

He leaned close again to whisper, switching now completely to sluttish French. "These treasures may be handed to your husband when he ascends the Chrysanthemum Throne, but everyone who is not woefully ignorant knows he's just a custodian on behalf of the — "

The Head Chamberlain interrupted himself in shock that he could, even in a Romance language, use such a term as "custodian" to describe the future father of the Japanese people. But the sentence on his tongue must be brought to full period, linguistic fastidiousness being characteristic of courtiers in all places and times. To compensate he got Teutonic.

" — on behalf of the Ewig Weibliche," he hawked, and translated unnecessarily: "The Eternal Feminine."

Crossing to the not-so-far wall, he began stroking and petting the various bric-a-brac on the bureau which the newlyweds were to share until Naruhito's accession, probably twenty or thirty

years in the future, when space would become a tad more plenti-
ful.

This chamber overflowed with evidence of the Royal
Family's unwholesome penchant for marine biology: mutated cat-
fish corpses, pickled jellyfish parts, white worms, sea slugs — so
many bottled atrocities. Shinto gods were to be conceived among
jars of lifeless and limp things. It was the occasion for a question
from a recent princessing lesson: "Which book of the holy Kojiki
refers to the 'slime like no other slime,' from which this august
lineage emerged?"

The Head Chamberlain fiddled thoughtfully with a large
specimen jar. It contained a black river snake that had, as its last
act on earth, gorged itself on a whole, snowy-white kitten. It had
then been split open with a scalpel and pinned wide to reveal its
lunch's furry little head, eyes surprised, bewildered and imploring,
among the fanned-out rib cage. The whole assemblage had been
lovingly floated in formaldehyde.

The Head Chamberlain took this sloshing qualm into his
arms and brought it to the foot of the floor mat. Owada didn't have
time to retract her feet before he plopped down.

With the jar nestled in his crossed legs, he began rocking
his stringy buttocks back and forth over her insteps, and saying
things like, "Have you ever watched that retired police matron out
there as she performs her duties at your feet? Is there a deeper look
of contentment to be seen on a primate face anywhere in Asia?
Don't you know that she'd be delighted to crawl on her belly
across molten asphalt for the privilege of opening a limousine door
for her Princess? Do you think she's odd? Far from it! Look hard
at her face sometime. It's the face of humanity — "

Milky tears began to uncoagulate from the crotches of his
lashless eyelids. "She's not only the happiest, but the realest and,
deep down, the most typical person either of us will ever know.
She knows where contentment lies: in service to the Gods. A life
of simple unquestioning service: That's the natural and perfect
condition for ninety nine-point-nine percent of homo sapiens, once
their vanity's been pulled down. Followed by still more full-time
service in rosy afterlife.

"Of course," he sighed deeply, starting to unscrew the lid of the jar, "you and I both know that Schopenhauer and the Hindus are right: When we die, it's like a glass of water being emptied into the ocean. But that's an insight the rank and file cannot be allowed access to. Look at the subcontinent. Do you want Japanese set adrift like that? Certainly not! Someone must provide them first with a functioning system of eschatological carrots and sticks, and then with a satisfactory object of devotion. Numinosity, I say, is all.

"Look at Europe. The dethroning of Mother Mary coincided with the end of the last golden age of the white races. Marx got the opiate part right, but he was disdainful rather than appreciative. People were awakened from the Edenic poppy dream, grew self-aware, and now everybody thinks he's entitled not to sweat or stink. Do you think it's a coincidence that the active ingredient in air conditioners and underarm deodorants is the very stuff that will cause the death of all life on the planet through ultra violet poisoning — the white races first among humans, which is only poetically just?

"When the Mother Goddess retires to her cave, pitiful pragmatism rushes in to supply the vacuum she leaves behind. And look at what it's done to these once-so-beautiful islands. The sea that was poured out from Heaven like good soup to feed us has become a sizzling basin of metallic toxins that twist and choke our babies. Even the skies are serrated with aluminous slivers and shards whose borrowed glare blots out more of our view of the sanctified stars each year. This orbiting junk gone ballistic already cracks the Americans' shuttle windows, and will soon make a simple spacewalk a suicide mission. It alone ensures we'll never escape the planet we've defiled like a diaper — which women have always known.

"But this, in itself, should be no cause for despair. People aren't a cancer on the earth; populist democracy is. That bit of male pride and puffery presupposes mass education, which requires mass prosperity, and we'll all suffocate on leaden smog long before that even begins to happen on a world-wide basis. What if every hundredth Chinaman who's been encouraged to lust after a car actually got one? Over the broad scope of human history, the middle class has been an ephemeral phenomenon, especially here in Asia, destined to dissolve. It's doing so, right now, apace, even in the United States. And well it should!

"Do you think the salary men of this archipelago lead anything like real lives in their stifling fluorescent-lit offices? Their souls are parched! Even the faintest, the most fleeting, the most rudimentary one-time-only glimpse of the Sublime that dwells beneath the maple veneer of their existence would cause them to fling their HDTVs and graphite golf clubs into the Pacific. They would follow this Sublime's numinous lead, straight to the gates of inconvenient, uncomfortable Hell if need be!

"Man needs to use his back muscles for something more than petty acts of purchased adultery and Sunday afternoon visits to the driving range. He yearns to have his vanity pulled down, his tired brain disburdened of the false cravings for 'self-actualization' foisted upon him by those flaming red, social-climbing, over-educated, Occidentalized rabble rousers who have infiltrated the Teacher's Union for fifty years. Oh, how the male of the species hankers after hard work that is directly and unambiguously tied to his own and his children's sustenance!

"The ideal disposition of human affairs has always been feudal aristocracy. And you can rest assured that the world will re-stabilize eventually in such a blessed medieval state, with or without our help: Ninety-nine-point-nine percent of the people drudging away at pre-industrial tilling methods, scratching nothing more nor less than their due carbohydrates, fiber by fiber, from the very dirt to which they contentedly return in the accidental form of replenishing corpses after no undue period. And everyone is kept happy in the meantime — not merely pacified, but truly fulfilled, their hearts and imaginations engaged — by a vigorous, and necessarily feminized religion. No need for mind-numbing pachinko parlors and jumbo-jets full of prepubescent Filipina sex slaves in such a regenerate society, where the Great Goddess has been reinstated.

"And you, good lady, are soon to be named the Spiritual Mother of the one industrialized nation that still has not completely lost track of these truths!

"The very surnames of our people shriek out for reunification with the soil. We have no Messrs. Baker, Smith or Glover. We have Messrs. Wide Field and Mountain Meadow. Much of our staple grain is grown by common salary men in their spare time on tiny plots of land with market values so hyperinflated that they could sell out tomorrow and retire to Golfers' Heaven, Arizona, leaving the rest of us to pick away at bowlfuls of imported Californian rice. But these salary men will never even briefly consider doing so. They'll never be voluntarily unlanded: For they are the ancestor-worshiping scions of families whose metaphysical destinies shall always remain inextricable from that asymmetrical little paddy they've nurtured and passed down for centuries.

"Owada-sama! Most fortunate Empress-to-be! Can't you see that most of your job is already done — or, rather, hasn't yet been undone? The donkey is saddled up, the palm fronds are strewn along the path, and the time is ripe for your triumphal ride into town! To make the trip a little easier, let us now rid ourselves of any superfluous emotional saddlebags, shall we? Yes we shall.

"I have gathered, from looking at your face whenever his name comes up — or, indeed, the name of anyone who could be remotely construed his representative — that relations between you and your male grandparent are, shall we say, severely strained of late. Am I right? Well, then you should stop pouting and welcome this mighty new apotheosis of yours! Hug it tight with all four youthful limbs! One would be hard-pressed to come up with a deeper and more thoroughgoing rejection of paternalism! Daddy and Grandpappy and Hubby, et al., may not know it, but you and I are going to turn the clock back to a time when people didn't even bother to memorize their fathers' stupid names!"

"But," interposed Owada, "if I act in disdain and bitterness, doesn't that negate, or at least vitiate — "

"Believe me, child. Your personal peeves are as gnat flatulence in the face of such a momentous task as the redemption of an entire people. Only a feminized religion can dissuade men from pampering and priding themselves into an ethical stupor, because it is based not on fuzzily focused faith in a featureless Father Figure, but on direct sensual experience of the immanent Numinous. And that can only be embodied satisfactorily in the smooth female form: Astarte, Ceres, Cybele, Demeter, Ishtar, Isis — to reckon merely a third of the foreigners' alphabet. These goddesses exert the ideal crowd control, and we must return to their bosoms. And so I can say this to you without qualification: the survival of the race depends upon you, personally, Owada-sama. For you are no exhibitionistic, blabber-mouthed, ruddy-mugged Windsor slut. You are, quite precisely, the only woman on earth to whom genuine numinosity is still available. You are the embodiment of the last true religion.

"An economical three-color print of your benevolent face will more than fill any vacancy left by a VCR. The strains of the devout chanting your name in the corner shrine will drown out, once and for all, the profane stridor of the karaoke bars. You see? Right there we've nearly halved the nation's electrical requirements!"

Focusing directly on her for the first time in several minutes, the Head Chamberlain gave off a broad wink. It was apparently an attempt to elicit a reaction to his joke.

"But," he said, sobering under her neutral gaze, "I can see the skeptical questions forming behind your eyes: Is this old dodderer talking about the redemption of the most productive and civil population on earth? What's to redeem? Did he use the phrase 'crowd control'? And did he speak of the invigoration of the numinous in the hearts of history's least religious people? How can a mere spiritual system — a womanly one at that — ever hope to wring even a mild sense of wonder from the Hollywoodized youth of today's Nippon? This frumpy old sycophant is babbling about alterations in the fundamental structure of the human psyche which would require millennia to effect. Or perhaps an across-the-board cataclysm, leaving only flattened, smoldering ground — scratch, as they say — from which to build up all afresh.

"Well, if Her Imperial Majesty will be so kind as to permit me to talk like a lowly fry cook: one across-the-board cataclysm, comin' right up!

"You've doubtlessly committed to heart all the prophecies of economic, social and environmental doom for our nation. Our bubble has indeed burst to smithereens, never to puff itself up again. Even as our decadent youth window-shop till they drop, the population grays at such an alarming rate that soon our proud Yamato blood will be tainted with that of the Gastarbeiter. Every one of our citizens but the pesky Okinawans lives well within the circle of Pyongyang's neophyte nuclear striking capability; and America intends, at any rate, to starve us all into submission with blustering blockades. Our sewage is sterilized by extravagant means while our precious paddies are pumped full of carcinogens that wring unrealistic yields from the expired soil; and the dread greenhouse effect will liquefy the polar caps tomorrow, anyway, leaving us with nothing to cultivate but oyster beds, which we'll guard jealously while bleating and clinging like goats to the upper crags of the few formerly lofty volcano tops that remain uninundated.

"Just so. I can swallow all of it. In your lifetime, my lady — and I cannot emphasize this strongly enough, so I will say it again, more loudly: in your lifetime, my lady, the Yamato tribe will be beaten and blasted to its knees, just as roundly as fifty years ago!

"But this time, when our humble and comely folk separate their tear-glued eyelids and look up in their agony, who will be there to meet their gaze? I can tell you right now that it won't be a corncob-sucking outlander, a fat-bottomed MacArthur, ready to bully a democratized delusion down their throats like a fifty-year-long overdose of noxious methedrine. No — "

The Head Chamberlain's eyes began to get circular, and his voice became rich, and it almost seemed as though the weight of his crotch lessened on her feet with each of the following ecstatic syllables.

" — they will behold none other than their own Princess, hovering at the eastern brink with, ah!, bright wings! Smooth and numinous in her Heian silks, gentle and soft-spoken in her persona, she shall glow with renewal in the old ways!

"Greed will succumb to quietism and a beatific annihilation of the will; consumerism will make way for prayer. Oh, it's going to be so nice around here! Thank you, Your Highness, for taking this heavy burden on your slim shoulders — though I realize, even if you, yourself, don't yet, that you are moved by forces greater than your own small will!"

At the mention of the substantive "will," the Head Chamberlain's face began to grow damp, and he lost control, predictably enough. Straightening of the spine and acceleration of the speech were his ways of achieving erection. He panted on awhile about the orgiastic side of this feminized religion: the temple prostitution, ritual castration, cannibalism and infant sacrifice — unpleasant but essential in the absence of the sacramental rationality which a male deity brings. But, as the entity whom this misbehavior was intended to propitiate, Owada could remain aloof. She did not have to listen to this part.

Instead, her heart began to writhe with a question. Finally it unglued itself from her tongue with a whisper: "But, Sensei, what about love?"

As if that question were some prearranged cue, Owada's babysitter / bodyguard slid open the shoji door from the outside, to the accompaniment of a shamisen being plunked and slammed by a tone-deaf toady in a neighboring chamber. The fanfare was apparently intended to underscore the entrance of somebody important. But in the odd, dim light it was impossible to tell who hesitated so diffidently in the former police matron's considerable shadow.

The Head Chamberlain was on his feet again, a man capable of not only intuitive, but also physical leaps. He escorted in someone half his height to take his place at the foot of the futon. Owada squinted to see whose bony knees were squashing her toes this time.

In the outlet next to her left ear was her Hello Kitty night light, the Prince's sole concession in the decor department. With regular changes of the bulb inside Kitty's skull, this tiny appliance had burned at her bedsides, both at home and abroad, for more than a quarter of a century. It had followed her here to the Togu Palace, surreptitiously tucked by grandfatherly hands in a bottom nook of her suitcase, along with a note she'd saved but never read. It chose this inauspicious moment to sputter and go out, depriving her eyes of its pinkish glow.

But, as if to compensate, the biological specimens began to exude the pale phosphorescence of decay from their respective jars and bottles. And it was by such an illumination that Owada recognized her life-mate.

The Prince knelt at her feet in full Heian bridegroom costume: a sandwich board of stiffened silk, the shoulders padded and bolstered wider by several centimeters than the height of the wearer. On his head was perched a little but still too-big cap whose front rim pushed and folded down a flap of scalp that impinged, in turn, upon his already low brow and brought an extra layer of sallow forehead flesh to bear upon his expressionless eyes, making them look even tinier than they were. The chin strap meanwhile puffed and pouted out his premature jowls. To provide a crowning glory for this sacred headdress, someone had thumb-tacked something like a shoehorn to the back of his skull. It was the long, flexible type designed to accommodate the lower-back problems of gerontocrats.

Even though she averted her eyes by automatic reflex, Owada knew what her husband solemnly fondled in the palm of his right hand. They clicked like miniaturized and very ineffective versions of the famous Japanese ben-wa, or joy balls.

Several months before, when his parents weren't home, he'd caused her to look at those very items. In an unauthorized dry run, Naruhito had insisted that she sneak with him into the very nerve-center of the Japanese state religion, the womb and font of the spiritual life of the Yamato tribe: the Most Inviolable, Taboo and Totally Sacred Chamber of the Royal Regalia.

She'd allowed herself to be led (but not by the hand) into that most holy-of-holies. She had watched her fiancé caress the grubby little things in one hand, while fiddling with his similarly withered gonads in the other — a younger-brotherly, yet joyless type of sex-play that would have turned her stomach even more than it had if she had only known just how aberrant it was outside the context of Japanese manhood.

The Sky Gods' gift to the Mother of Humanity, these genuine and original Curved Jewels were, as far as Owada had been able to ascertain in the gloomy closet, a couple of lumps of dimly discolored quartzite shellacked to look like jade. Their false surfaces had been rendered dull and grainy by the obeisances of a few millennia's worth of devout fingers' skin oils. Shaped like soixante-neuf with terminal coitus interruptus, Yin and Yang pried apart, Aristophanes' fancy: two alienated halves of a former hermaphroditic whole, divided by a curve of the same amplitude as the incriminating cut in Julius and Ethel Rosenberg's Jello box, which sent them, male and female, two by two, to their separate but equal dooms.

And so Owada had the answer to her question. This was love for the Empress of Japan: the very least of her duties.

Gagging on silent giggles all the while, the Head Chamberlain now performed campy mumbo-jumbo over the Prince's uncomprehending, but, as always, smug head. The old trickster flitted behind his future Lord and Sovereign and pretended to whang the shoehorn like the string of a washtub bass. He leaned his chin on the Son of Heaven's broadened shoulder and made pompous toad faces at the bedded but unbreached bride. It looked as though he were about to anoint the spawn of Hirohito with crumby formaldehyde from the snake-and-kitty jar. Was this yet another time-honored Shintoist sacramental rite, or was Owada's re-educator just improvising?

"Love and work, cashews and commas, ooga-boo" the old man chanted. He snickered awhile, catching drunken mirth in his withered right palm. Then his swirling eyes focused on his darling protégé, and saw something in her face than made him frown and grow a bit pettish.

"Oh, please, you mustn't despair," he said, in a loud voice, in one or another of the several languages her husband would never know. "This mooncalf is irrelevant. After all, Snuggles," (he called her that whenever his Confucian screen dropped completely away, and he became a gossipy, wrist-patting old woman — pure English now) "it's your blood, the thick sauce that infuses your supple limbs — I imagine it scrubbing against the interior walls of your young capillaries, almost gritty with bits of wholesome iron and all the right minerals, sifting and shifting like Tottori dunesand — that's going to produce a viable heir, not his milky turquoise piss.

"And, inexpressibly more important than coughing up this viable heir you've been hearing so much about, will be your duty to strike out into the wilderness of Tokyo and unearth yourself a good daughter-in law. And I mean a really good one! When Sho-wa-tenno's mother, the grand Empress Temei, manifested her auspicious self at the Gakushuin School for Female Peers and selected the current Empress-Dowager from among the blushing ranks of pre-screened and -selected candidates, do you suppose she was performing work of less than the uttermost cosmic significance? Well, suppose otherwise! Love itself" (gesturing dismissively down at Naruhito) "pales and withers in comparison; it reduces to a recipe of fluids and friction.

"When we release your official wedding photos to every wire service and TV network in the free world, do you think anybody's going to glance at this plucked rat in his pathetic clown suit? Of course not! If there's to be numinosity, it must exude from your half of the frame. And it will, Love, it will.

"Speaking of which, I do believe it's time for the hands-on portion of our little night tutorial. It's time for a certain somebody I know to mount the wooden turntable that will spin her back to the Golden Age of our civilization!"

When Owada hesitated (her bridegroom still knelt dumbly on her toes), the Head Chamberlain got just a little impatient — but not enough to spoil the mood. He said, "Come, come. Shall we go? Since yours is a very special case, I think we can put this much-touted 'bridal breach' nonsense off for a more convenient time. Just elbow that bony-assed twit aside. No need to get dressed. Rest assured that we will do that for you from now on! The Americans say, 'Rise and shine.' Well, I say the same to you now, in a sense as nearly literal as possible. Rise, my Princess, and do shine!"

Fatted Calf

But as soon as this thy son was come,
which hath devoured thy living with harlots,
thou hast killed for him the fatted calf.
—Luke 15:30

"words, sounds...whatever!" (impishly printed with no capitalized letters) was a retail outlet that specialized in the sale of sheet music for "sacred songs," i.e., vocal works stylistically somewhat more secular than your bona fide hymns, yet dealing with uplifting sentiments, mostly exhorting you to let Christ be your role model.

And this is where my acknowledged Euterpean gifts came in handy. My favorite cousin, the handsome and semi-consciously gay Bryce Barkdull, was the owner/proprietor of the establishment, and he was overjoyed to have me as an employee. He stationed me in the sheet music section as a salesman/demonstrator, with my concert-grand Lyon-Healy harp and my not-too-shabby bass-baritone voice.

I would sit there, swathed in a silken pharaoh shirt supplied by Bryce. Upon request I dashed off, at first sight, pretty bad piano arrangements, admittedly looking incongruous in such a place, among such pious folk. But that was the whole point, the beauty of the situation. I was the mascot, if you will. With the threat of the mobilized sixties long since dissipated, shaggy dogs like me were anachronistic and whimsical.

As a matter of fact, we two cousins had a running joke, good for laughs often, that drew upon my "different" image:

Bryce would greet a customer with something like, "Well, Brother (such-and-such), it's so agreeable to behold your radiant countenance!" And I would grunt, "Yeah, and it's nice to see your shiny face, too."

See? Everybody would beam fondly at my long red beard, and say, "Isn't he just a terrible guy?"

Another example:

One bright Friday we were patronized by Elder Cicerone, the father of a certain young ex-missionary who regularly attempted to perpetrate murder and cannibalism and sodomy, and so forth, upon various youngsters in the neighborhood.

Elder Cicerone was the august, capable type of Mormon, at home in the world of affairs, and unembarrassed by the more unscientific tenets of his church. Elder Cicerone told you with his eyes that he was familiar with Marx's famous likening of religion to analgesic widely administered; but he would not deign respond. His tight-lippedness on theological issues was justified by his having chosen to reside in the United States of America, where the First Amendment has guaranteed that religion shall be the point at which all critical activity ceases in the public mind.

The Elder realized that cynics would leap at the chance to twist his mode of worship into a source of personal or professional chagrin, if he were ever to acknowledge the remote possibility that a word or phrase might someday be ferreted from the back pages of the Prophet Fathers' books that could discomfit a rational Mormon. What unsaved heathens had to say about his mighty church miffed Elder Cicerone not in the slightest.

Even when scandal-mongering Christ-baiters tried to pick away at the slight irregularities in his personal life, it did not shake the composure of such a serene, influential man as Elder Cicerone.

Let the out-of-towners slither up in their foreign cars, to preach false doctrine from the wine-sticky pool decks of the local "Gentile" tourist resort. Let them besottedly insinuate that the Elder had converted and immigrated because he saw bucks to be made among people who were, by definition, gullible and sheepish. It failed to ripple the calm lake of composure that was his soul; for he had faith in Christ-Jesus, the Almighty, the Son of Man.

When slavering demoniacs hissed rumors abroad, outright misrepresentations of fact, about the young ex-missionary with whom he shared his home, suggesting that the Elder had wielded his religious (therefore, in Utah, political) clout to gain clemency for that misbegotten boy, unmiffed is how the old man remained.

Like many businessmen who have chosen to live out their lives under great financial and moral pressure, Elder Cicerone had his inner turbulencies, to be sure. He was only human—contrary to the suspicions of several inhabitants of this valley. But he was able to sublimate with a single, harmless, playful gesture, once a year, when he squirted the peasants with his gigantic alfalfa sprinklers at the Good and Lucky Festival of the Sugar Beet Harvest. It was just a hint of human foible in his otherwise transcendent life.

And the humble folk put up with it, assuming it was par for this particularly weird course: "We don't get a whole lotta Eyetie converts in this neck o' the dang woods," they'd mutter, wringing non-potable orange fluids from their calico and gingham.

An "Eyetie convert" was exactly what he called himself, with pride. He'd been re-baptized by full immersion, in middle age, in the middle Mediterranean. He'd immigrated first to New Jersey, the idea having been to rear his son on the east coast, to take advantage of the superior educational and cultural resources available there; then to make the pilgrimage to this mountain Mecca, here to relocate and remain, close at hand, to assist in the more recondite operations of his newly found faith.

The Elder wore a pony tail, a short, tucked-in silver one, to make his handsome old self appear even more patriarchal. Though his closest relatives were either dying or being born in Sicily, his ultimate blood lines hailed from the crisp shores of Lake Como, at the broad base of the Alps; and he looked as though he could be cousin to any one of the many Swiss converts who gorgeously marched the streets of Salt Lake City: broad, tall and fair.

But the Elder's son, the badly-behaved ex-missionary (Streckfuss happened to be his very peculiar name) was one-hundred-percent skinny dago. Were it not for an incongruous shock of Titian-red hair, the late Adolf Eichmann might have left-handedly complimented the boy by calling him "latterly darkened."

The Elder was able, when expedient, to cover his native accent with a brilliant and consistent imitation of a bucktoothed, adenoidal Intermountain twang, for he'd enjoyed decades of experience in applied linguistics in the blood-bathed back alleys of Palermo and, later, Camden. But Streckfus, having inherited neither his father's ear nor supple tongue, forever whined like the eastern seaboard guinea he was.

Now, whenever new titles issued from the prolific pens of the august Mormon leadership, the Elder would make a prompt visitation upon "words, sounds...whatever!" in order to purchase them as gifts for his beloved son, who claimed to "dig where the old cats was coming from." Politically and theologically, the church leadership and Streckfuss seemed to share a wavelength.

So, on this one sunny payday, when I was lucky enough to be seated at the toilet rather than the harp, far from the phone, Streckfuss, who shunned ultraviolet radiation, had called ahead on his old man's behalf to make sure a new shipment of such tracts had arrived. He had initiated a literary discussion of sorts with Bryce on the subject of a certain Councilor's works. Midway through the call, the squeaky little voice on the other end of the line had made the perceptive observation that the Councilor's style betrayed the kind of unresolved emotional problems usually found in men one fourth his age.

"Maybe unlucky in love," Streckfuss had suggested, momentarily choking up—or so my cousin swore, with a shudder, upon my fragrant return.

But the shudder had been a slight one. For Bryce Barkdull enjoyed professional identity, that ultimate solidifier of character, several times more potent than mere sexual identity. Even a telephonic confrontation with our home-grown version of Jeffrey Dahmer didn't faze him too badly.

In any case, later that afternoon, Elder Cicerone, father of Streckfuss and the holder of an elevated, if shadowy status within the hierarchy of the Church, dropped by my sheet music counter on his way to pay for some pamphlets on the subject of the "twin Trotskyite conspiracies" of Medicare and bilingual education. The

Elder browsed awhile at my perspiring elbow, then selected a popular item that had just come in.

"I dearly love this with all my heart, and intend to master it on our Color-Glo Organ in time for my boy's upcoming birthday!" frankly beamed the healthy-faced old gentleman. "Can you show me how it is supposed to sound, old Mr. Sambo?" (That was my nickname around the shop—don't even ask how it got started.)

Well, old Mr. Sambo somehow forced his eyeballs to stop swirling long enough to give the thing a quick preliminary scan. It was composed by the epic poet of an entire generation, old Mr. Bob Dylan, not long after that fine entertainer's precipitous plunge into aged celebrityhood, early personality disintegration, amphetamine-induced brain damage, and, finally, and most tragically, born-again Christianity. This tune featured a Latin, or bossa nova-type flair; but, like all of the master's works, it was couched in solid, three-note Caucasian harmonies, nothing too hard to pluck out with horror-quaking fingers.

I rendered this song, which was entitled, simply, "The Prodigal Son":

O Prodigal Son, my Prodigal Son,
You been lost and won
My Prodigal Son.
No more will you run
My Prodigal Son.
There's a place in the sun
For Prodigal Son.
You're the only one,
My Prodigal Son.
I'll no longer shun
My Prodigal Son.
See the fatted-calf juices run,
My Prodigal Son?
Pass the hot dog bun
My Prodigal Son, O Prodigal Son,
Yes Prodigal Son, I said Prodigal Son.
Yeah-yeah-yeah Prodigal Son.
No-no-no Prodigal Son.
Oh baby-baby, Prodigal Son.

Hear me talking to ya, Prodigal Son?
Prodigal Son, my Prodigal Son.

Mesmerized by the unrelenting inventiveness of the lyrics, I forgot, for an entire measure, my trepidation. I was able to interpolate that bit about the hot dog bun into this masterpiece by the living legend from Duluth. My audience was shocked by the utter irreverence, but eventually recovered.

"Isn't he the most terrible guy?" Elder Cicerone asked Bryce after a moment of stunned silence.

My employer beamed heartily. Cousin Bryce jingled the register, keeping time with me, and slipped sheet music in bags, all the while brimming with the accumulated warmth of a bosom friendship that had continued for almost twenty-five years: through the shared intimacies of our babyhood to the indiscretions of our teenhood, first intercourse, first LSD, first night in jail, and now, thanks be to the intercession of the Divine Paraclete, to the venture capitalism of our adulthood.

Bryce said, "Yea verily," or something like that, and, with warmth, thumped the father of Streckfuss on his broadened shoulder.

See? Yet another example of how I, bearded Sambo, my exotic joyful-noisemaker snuggled between my thighs, served as the resident character of "words, sounds...whatever!"

Very good, old Mr. Sambo!

Harsh Words of Mercury

Pity the Japanese woman who thinks bleak thoughts every time silvery water presents itself to her eye. She's like a sparrow reminded of steel wool when it bellies into a cloud.

Sui-gin, "water silver": the imagistic way her native tongue denoted a certain substance. She'd long since forgotten the term for it in Russian (probably an English cognate). This heavy, shiny, rolling gunk was like no other liquid her kindergarten classmates had ever run between their fingers and fondled in palms with all the scrapes, vermin bites and unnamed sores of active, normal, marginally nourished Soviet childhood.

And among the pink hands were a few yellow ones, equally permeable. One pair belonged to an embassy brat with a large number of air miles already under her belt, a girl from an isle of bourgeois capitalism in the seas beyond Siberia. Her hands, in retrospect, were even scrawnier than those which would almost bungle the elementary school entrance examination a year later, back in Tokyo. Little Masako was a hyper-adrenalized nail biter even at that tender age, so there was no shortage of exposed quick and peeled-back hangnails on her microscopic fingertips. Plenty of holes and lesions for the juicy metal to seep into.

Their instructor, one Comrade Svidrigailov, was a gigantic snow-colored person, a failed applicant for admission to the Central Institute for Advanced Technology. She wanted her young charges never to be frustrated as she'd been. When not seated at the twelve-ton cast-iron spinet accompanying unsyncopated songs in minor keys (nothing like the dozens of happy-go-lucky Portuguese ditties Masako had memorized in her Brasilia nursery school), Comrade Svidrigailov concentrated on providing the children with an intensive introduction to the wonders of science. She called it her modest contribution to the arms race with America, then in full swing.

She'd already demonstrated the phenomenal effects of liquid nitrogen: a downright circus of rubber balls exploding like light bulbs, whole reams of construction paper shattering like so many panes of glass, nails being hammered deep into concrete with the help of roughly cylindrical food items (which reconstituted themselves in Masako's memory as overripe bananas, but had probably been large barrel-pickled turnips). The whole extravaganza had been a major success, eliciting the only response Comrade Svidrigailov had ever gotten from the natty scions of rich party muckamucks in the front row. A few eyelids had even stirred among the otherwise feral communards and hereditary muzhiks in the back.

Aberrant substances seeming to get through to young minds where the mere language of Pushkin failed, Comrade Svidrigailov decided to try a similar approach again. Hydrochloric acid was her dream, for it would lead into many edifying discussions of the human digestive system, not to mention the intimidation techniques of gangsters in capitalist countries. But sulfuric acid was hard to come by, unlike her second choice of substances. And her second choice, as far as she was aware, was a lot less hazardous to handle.

So she used a change for the worse in the already terrible weather as a heavy-handed segue to a new topic in the science unit. She brought in a couple of baby thermometers, the intrusive occidental style. Not forgetting to field and pitch the expected jokes about the glass knob on the business end (Bolsheviks seemed to find in anuses a much richer source of humor than do Japanese—or at least Japanese of the governing class), she broke them open and, placing a dab on each little desk, invited the children to "get familiar" with the contents.

Warming to the occasion with the first hoots of ecstasy from the front row, Comrade Svidrigailov climbed on top of her own desk and revealed the dazzling way the nectar under consideration splashed and splintered into a million eyeball-grazing globules when allowed to drop from a height.

"But watch out for the broken glass. It's dangerous."

Masako hesitated to handle the stuff. It seemed not to belong within her range of experience, this liquid that hefted like a solid. A native of relatively balmy Honshu Island, she was still sorting out the relationship between the hard slippery material that clogged Moscow's gutters and the burning clouds that belched from the omnipresent samovars. But she allowed herself to be peer-pressured into participating in this "science project" because she thought it might be a good way to do what she was always urged to do by her mom, a former stewardess with Air France, where they'd mis-nicknamed her "China Doll" and printed her name tags accordingly for the decade-plus she'd flown with them.

"Find what it is about yourself," Mom said, "that might incite confusion or disharmonious feelings, and smooth it over." Open yourself wide like a lotus blossom and smile as you assimilate whatever metals they feel like forcing into your body.

Father must not have listened to such admonitions. After putting in more than a month of overtime, when he didn't get home at his usual hour of eleven o'clock but stayed in the embassy all night, catching a cat nap here and there, he finally managed to finagle an evening off to pay an uninvited visit to the party cell of the school board and raise holy Buddhist Hell about toxins in the classroom. Mom fastened her fingernails into his shoulder and tried to hold him back, pleading, "Father! Don't cause a scene! Don't shame us by making a nuisance of yourself! We're guests in this country, as I keep telling your brain-damaged daughter!"

Mom turned out to be right—not about brain damage, but about being a nuisance. Reprisal for the disturbance was immediate. Daddy's daughter was accosted the very next day by older kids from the upstairs grammar school, red-scarved Young Pioneers and Junior Socialist Leaguers.

"Do your bones get any longer when the temperature rises in the summer?" they chortled around chronically swollen adenoids and tonsils. "You could use the extra height."

Of course, she had no idea what they were talking about. She was only able to interpret this treatment as bullying by squinting hard, and almost straight up, into their dazzling white faces, where she instinctively recognized broad sneers of sadistic glee.

They enticed her into the reading room and caused her to look at Chapter Three of their mimeographed Cyrillic primer, Exploitation of the Proletariat Throughout the World. The illustrations were pirated from an old Look Magazine expose, and featured people who looked something like the scattered few Mongolian types in her class. Gifted Masako was already able to muddle through the few English captions that hadn't been cropped by the commissars, and they said the people in the pictures were actually Japanese. It followed that their faces must also have resembled her own, even though she'd lately been feeling quite white among all the vast Slavs.

Before being shown the Look photos, Masako had harbored only the vaguest suspicions as to why everybody, especially Comrade Svidrigailov, expected her to associate exclusively with the strange kids from out east. Barely able to speak, those eyeless outcastes were bused, or rather trekked in all the way from Irkutsk for ideological purposes, and to preserve correct appearances in this model school. They tended not to be the most exciting playmates in Eurasia, as they spent a lot of time gazing wistfully up into the sunless sky, tears streaming down their round faces.

But now it finally dawned on Masako that she'd been encouraged to find a desk among their unwashed ranks solely in consideration of the physical features she shared with them. With the strange objectivity of the very young, she began dispassionately to question the beauty that Daddy, if not Mommy, always claimed to see in her face.

Her Caucasoid classmates' gold, ivory and lapis-lazuli kissers were the very models for Likka-chan, the Shinjuku high-fashion doll. Masako and every other Japanese girl owned and loved Likka-chan, built whole inner worlds around her, and laid the foundations of their psyches on her escape-and-rescue adventures, co-starring similarly melanin-unencumbered plastic princes, sold separately. Once Masako had idly wondered aloud, within Mother's earshot, whether black-haired, almond-eyed dolls were manufactured anywhere in the world, and had gotten nothing but a blank stare, a silent pause, then a bemused chuckle, followed gently by, "Don't try to tell jokes. Humor is a difficult trick even for a male. You certainly haven't the intelligence for it."

The oriental faces in the Look expose were among the few this tiny expatriate had ever seen depicted in something other than restaurant advertisements, and she examined them with interest, trying to learn about herself.

But all was not well with this particular bunch of Asians. They looked to be simple fishermen and their families, but were twisted and wadded like botched origami sculptures: limbs bent backward, eyeballs charlie-horsed, tongues lolled in square knots. Putting the best face on an unpleasant situation, as all good Nihonjin do, several of the less sorely afflicted in one photo tried to enjoy a hot bath together with their offspring. (The polar children hovering over Masako's shoulder giggled at least as much at the hairless nakedness as at the pain.) Through mimeographed steam, Masako's countrymen gazed with love into their sons' and daughters' unrecognizable, unrecognizing eyes.

In another picture she saw the administrative building of a nearby chemical plant, secure behind a living cordon of sumo-sized riot policemen. It was hard to believe that the blue-clad officers were born of the same stock as the withered and wasted freaks who swooned and waved protest signs among poison-vomiting culverts on the other side of the chain-link fence. And, though she didn't let on at the time, Masako was already able to read the Romanized name of her grandfather's corporation in the captions.

As if on cue, Comrade Svidrigailov chose that moment to stride into the lime-green reading room. At a glance she was able to see her proper course of action. The leaders deemed her unqualified to be placed in charge of the older pupils' nurture under normal circumstances; but this was a rare opportunity to exploit the special foreign student as a living, blushing object lesson.

"Have you looked into those people's eyes?" boomed Comrade Svidrigailov in her mannish voice. "The expression has been skewed not only by degeneration of the tissue underlying the eyelids, but by dissolution of the central nervous system. Their very senses were being perverted, therefore the universe itself was perverted, as far as they were able to ascertain. And their perceptions had just enough time to drive them insane with terror before the pure physical agony killed them. It would be very hard, my children, to imagine a more unpleasant way to leave this earth."

(A pause to wink broadly at the meanest sixth-grade boys, the sharp dressing sophisticates with well-connected fathers, to whose French-wine-and-American-movie parties this social-climbing educator cherished faint hopes of being invited.)

"A certain young lady's family," continued Comrade Svidrigailov, "under the kind auspices of Japan's mighty Chisso Corporation, enriched those poor fish-workers' water with plenty of the runny silver which my kindergartners just studied. And, as you can see, it did not have the best effect on their general level of health, for they put it in their mouths, not just their hands. You didn't take a sip, did you, Comrade Masako?"

Titters were heard from a small mob gathering in the reading room. Comrade Svidrigailov possessed the emotional maturity of the least grown-up of them, but was better informed. So when she instigated the taunting, she was able to bring a more or less adult sting to it.

"Now I'm not saying there's any definite scientific connection. But the owners and operators of the offending plant, being rich enough to consume more than their fair share of the local catch, might develop a resistance to the disease. And you know there's a genetic component to class. Lenin said so. And capitalist exploiters do tend to produce a certain type of offspring..."

"Resistance?" snickered Anna Belov, whose little sister Masako had always fancied to be a borderline friend. "That must be why this Nip's face is only slightly lopsided, like the American WC Fields'."

"Yes," chimed in another behemoth kid. "She talks out of one side. A natural water carrier for a basketball team. She can pass on contraband instructions from the coach."

"Or she could be one of those interpreters that cower and mumble at the Jap emperor's elbow all day long."

"She's born for it."

"Interpreter, nothing. She acts like a princess herself."

"What about the slitty eyes? Did the thermometer juice cause that affliction?"

"They're all cursed with such eyes."

"The stuff must palsy the hands as well. That's why she's got such putrid handwriting."

"And, please don't forget, its atomic number is 200.59," Comrade Svidrigailov reminded everybody, deftly steering the discourse back onto the scientific track now that political obligations had been fulfilled.

Branded the justifiably tormentable spawn of black-class bourgeois reactionaries, Masako came home crying daily over the course of an entire semester. She was politely ignored until she started to disturb the downstairs neighbors' rest with screaming nightmares about her arms bending backward at the elbows and shattering like thermometers.

"Amend your ways," said Mom, finally, bedside, in a relatively soothing tone. It was deep night in their cavernous Moscow flat. Daddy was still at work, and Masako had just turned in a contemptible performance on the times-thirteen multiplication table. "You must work hard to learn what it is about yourself that provokes such discord among your coevals," said Mom. "And correct it promptly before any more disharmony results from this weakness of yours, whatever it may be."

At that, the little girl's weeping got louder, and Mother continued her comments, unperturbed.

"There, there. I know it's hard to make yourself into a good citizen. But we must learn to put the best face on everything. Every experience has a silver sheen to it, if you've been born with enough basic intelligence to peer closely around the edges. We must fix on the good side. Your pain today will make you a better member of society tomorrow."

Mother shifted onto the other buttock and said, in a bedtime-story voice, "Once, when I was a stewardess, I allowed myself to be caught unawares by a pocket of clear-air turbulence and popped an upper vertebra on the cabin ceiling, starboard, aft. I was forced to remain supine for the remainder of the flight, not only depriving my fellow crew members of my help, but taking up precious space on the galley floor. And do you know what I did?"

Sleepy Masako didn't leap to reply, so Mom put the question again, more firmly—but first asking the child, rhetorically, of course, whether she'd been born with no eardrums as well as no penis and no cerebral cortex.

"What did you do?" asked Masako.

"Well, I'll tell you. The second I got out of the hospital—even though my co-workers were all foreigners and therefore congenitally incapable of forming even a rudimentary idea of what I was doing—I removed my shoes and kowtowed to them ten times in the Air France stewardesses' central lounge, five-kilo neck brace and all."

"Was that in wonderful, beautiful Paris?"

"Not that it matters, but yes. Shall we review our Periodic Table of Elements now? What comes right after gold?"

"In our family?" asked Masako, and got a prompt good-night slap in return.

From that point on, the child began asking herself what good it would do to amend her ways when her sin was inherited, according not only to her teacher, but to the mean boys who got her alone in the stairwell and teased her in a dialect she comprehended only imperfectly.

"Your whole family," they said, "lives on the flesh of fishermen scooped dead from the silver sludge of Minamata Bay."

Little Masako began to weep into her pillow every night, more fiercely, in anger now as well as heartbreak. She only wanted to be friends with people, and the big kids were inciting even the token Uzbeks to shun her.

"That's just because they think you're an egghead," explained Dad one Sunday afternoon while she scrubbed his back. It was just the two of them awash in the white man-sized bathtub, an unprecedented treat, for her sisters were taking naps. He was speaking softly so his voice wouldn't bounce off the tile walls and into the kitchen. It would be better if Mom didn't hear him putting immodest sentiments inside her head.

"It's just because you can read two and a half languages already in kindergarten, and it's plain to see that you're going to learn more and more. Even your ridiculous teacher feels inadequate in front of you. That's the real reason everybody's so mean. The Minamata matter is just a smoke screen, a false charge trumped up by communists ashamed of their own mediocrity."

He looked up at the steamy light fixture, which might very well have been bugged, and added, in a much louder voice, "Petty envy is the crippling curse of the Marxist dispensation!"

* * * *

But, a year later, back home in Nippon, "the Minamata matter" was exactly what a certain six-year-old would think she saw, caked and bursting from the hollows of a heat-split skeleton at a hillside crematorium. It was a special afternoon, when she was allowed to publicly display her dinner-table skills for the first time.

Masako had been pressed to early chopstick mastery by— who else? Mom believed, along with many of her compatriots, that such digital discipline, reinforced by its intimate connection with sustenance, somehow enhanced one's mathematical aptitude.

"Eating our rice with a pair of hashi from childhood on," explained Mom, "loosens up our built-in abacus. What do I mean by such a cryptic remark? Well, I'll tell you. We Nihonjin, in ancient times, perfected the secret art of using our fingers in calculating. Hence the discrepancy in math scores between our high school enrollees and the spoon-wielding barbarians on the far side of the Pacific. Here, fool, let me show you."

She grabbed Masako's hand and commenced dislocating digits.

"Thumb into the palm is one, followed by the index, two, and so on and so forth, until all four fingers have cloaked the thumb in an attitude unsuited for fist fighting."

(Later, as a student in Boston, Masako would learn that the number-five position was the male homosexual salute. It had seemed significant at the time, but she'd meanwhile forgotten how.)

In the event, Masako was able to hone these exquisite skills to the point where she was allowed to help her extended family pick through the few chunks of an unmarried old relative which had survived the consecrated incinerator—all according to the venerable traditions of her ancestral Buddhist sect.

Mother explained that, macabre as this ritual would seem to foreigners, the burnt bone-picking served a definite theological purpose in certain segments of Japanese society. It was a kind of inchoate Eucharist for closet ancestor-worshippers, a tip of the Buddhist hat to Nihonjin who might otherwise be disinclined to profess a foreign faith imported third-hand from the Asian mainland.

Masako's Daddy had given her a brand-new kid-sized black sequined clutch purse to go with the rest of her mourning outfit. To impress Mom with how well she was able to plan ahead and equip herself in advance, she had tucked into that purse her pretty new Hello Kitty chopsticks with the real moving eyes.

But Mom only wound up ridiculing her (in a whisper, of course) because, as anybody but a mongoloid cretin would know, crematoria provide their own chopsticks for the special task, cooking size, green and white ivory, to be left sticking upright among the beloved's remains in exactly the position which one was never, ever to leave one's regular hashi sticking in rice, because of the morbid (read unlucky) associations.

"I'm certain Great Auntie wouldn't appreciate being culled from this ash trough and placed into the memorial urn by cartoon character hashi," sneered Mom as they knelt with cousins and grannies around the sirloin-fragrant pit.

She paused to critically appraise her daughter's dishwashing job, then added, in a dour tone, "Especially not with a solidified grain of rice adhering to the left one. In any case, that chunk's too big to retrieve with chopsticks. Even if you were a sturdy boy and the pride of our household, you wouldn't have the finger muscles to do it. Nobody expects you to even try. It's foolish, as well as immodest and disruptive to the social order, for a dull girl like you to be such an overachiever. Content yourself with this wrist bone—and what's the New Latin term for it?"

In the vestibule of the Buddhist funeral parlor, Masako had watched her dutiful dad bop his fine mahogany-brown forehead on the floor at the feet of each well-wisher and condolence deliverer, including some uninvited ones: fishermen from the newly condemned bay—perfectly well-behaved, as their presence alone was disruption enough.

Shadow-lurking Minamata Grampa, having just lost a sister to more natural causes than they'd lost theirs, addressed a beautiful young monk in a whisper audible clear across the reception area, even over the roaring of the stoked furnace. He grumblingly described the unwashed intruders as "cheeky opportunists whose own genes can't produce worthy heirs, so they invent a scandal, cast aspersions on our pristine effluents, and try to tap the corporation for settlements—less euphemistically known as blood money—to finance them as they mop up after their deformed children. Well, they won't see a single aluminum yen from it! Not in my lifetime, by God!"

"I imagine not in theirs, either," murmured the monk as he surveyed the quaking, gasping interlopers.

At their twisted feet, meanwhile, Daddy kowtowed especially hard on the concrete, as if to drown out Grampy's unrepentant words, his skull sounding full of thickish fluid and about to burst like a shrunk-wrapped honeydew. And that was the first time Masako saw her loving Father's face crumple, his character, by all visible indications, sink into temporary but total disarray.

It was a measure of how little this sort of thing is talked about in polite Japanese society that she had to wait until she entered junior high school and enrolled in an AP biology course to find out that infection with the "Minamata matter" wasn't really hereditary at all. And even then she figured it out for herself, using an American textbook her father had brought home from the US Consulate library. Masako's biology teacher hadn't enough common scientific sense even to understand the question, and couldn't imagine why he should: nothing like it was scheduled to appear on any college entrance exams.

Speaking of such all-important examinations, already at the age of six Masako had been drilled by Mom in anatomy and several other morally unambiguous disciplines whose essences could be reduced to basic response conditioners, such as systems of flash cards. Nevertheless, with the enormous amounts of other information that had been compacted between the walls of her skull since that afternoon at the hillside ovens, Masako could not be sure that she'd correctly identified (had she identified it out loud?) a large, blackened, slightly greasy object as a femur.

Great Auntie's thigh bone—which, she hoped, smelled like an out-house only in retrospect—had split wide open in the flames, and little Masako had seen, or thought she'd seen, oozing from where the barbecued marrow should've oozed, a certain liquescent sub-stance, that terrible sauce, the curse of her clan.

The roasted marrow had seemed silvery, and she couldn't help thinking of the etymology of sui-gin. Her skeleton loaded with such gunk, Great Auntie would've indeed gotten taller, which is to say, better, worthier of love, had she survived into summer.

Flip

Mr. Fukuoka was one congenital Shintoist who could not abide the reek of incense. Three birthdays of his boyhood had been asphyxiated by the rank stuff, starting with his tenth: April 24, 1942, which was exactly one chaotic, humiliating, world-destroying month after FDR signed executive order number 9066. This piece of paper allowed the Secretary of War to designate the entire west coast of the United States a "militarily sensitive area," from which "any persons (read nips) could be excluded."

The Fukuoka family had been driven from the groves of northern California, whose gentle hills and rivulets of sweet water had more or less comfortably harbored his homesick parents' thousands of Shinto deities. And they landed in a concentration camp near Topaz Mountain, in the orange and white desert of deepest Utah.

Dispossessed of virtually everything, but most reluctantly of her joss sticks, Fukuoka's mother had to make do with some loose, smelly grains of a medium-grade Papist manufacture. In what he called a political act, Fukuoka's older brother had liberated several boxfuls from the jeep of a chaplain who descended weekly into hell for the dispensation of something facetiously called a benediction.

Okaa-san fastened onto her older son's combustible gift, and proceeded systematically to neglect, then abandon her younger son outright, the better to adulterate with smoky magic the single wholesome aspect of the otherwise miserable place to which they'd been transported.

Today, Fukuoka found himself unable to imagine, much less remember, the few puffs of that healing desert atmosphere, arid, limpid, and sage pungent, which his boyish lungs had been permitted to inhale free of the sickly perfumes of propitiation.

Born citizens of the right age and political leanings could emerge from behind the barb wire a few afternoons a week to attend classes at the local junior college, one of the worst in the entire free world. For those unwilling to submit to the racist jibes of the backwater professors, the War Relocation Authority had another offer. They showed up in camp with their turquoise megaphones, and, along with facile apologies for exceeding their authority in detaining "conceded loyals," they blasted out prerecorded propaganda, aimed especially at the young nisei, about vast economic opportunities in places like Oklahoma, and offering permanent leave clearances to anyone willing to resettle in the midwest or east.

Then came the most unrefusable offer of all for the few young men, like Fukuoka's older brother, who wouldn't allow themselves to be reeducated in cow colleges or deported even further away from California, which they considered their rightful home: the draft finally found its way to the relocation center. Rather than being packed off to Europe in a brigade of second-generation nips and placed on the front lines to see if any Nazis would shoot, Older Brother promptly started a one-man resistance movement.

For all the photos he'd saved, it wasn't until well into middle age that Fukuoka was able to remember what Older Brother had looked like in those courageous days. At the time, Fukuoka's Hollywood-saturated eyes could not see properly. His half-formed, boyish brain had lacked some inner apparatus for recognizing an oriental male who didn't wear Coke bottle glasses and suck voraciously on a set of buck teeth that hung down past an Adam's apple pointed and protuberant as the prow of a mackerel boat; who wasn't treacherous, cringing or bloodthirsty, but straightforward, vigorous and kind. In short, all-American: a kind of compact, long waisted Erroll Flynn with almond eyes and no facial hair.

Fukuoka always wondered whether his big brother had been able to apprehend his own beautiful self as he dashed about in the dry night air, performing stalwart acts of subversion, sabotage and requisitioning. In any case, for his gift of frankincense to

Okaa-san, Older Brother was tried, convicted and sent back homeward after all, to California's Tule Lake Camp, reserved for troublemakers, thence to the federal penitentiary on Alcatraz.

Mother's response was not to take advantage of whatever vestigial legal recourse remained to people of their kind, but to hunker even further down into her dowdy labyrinth of superstition. She improvised a family shrine from the only things resembling lumber to be found in that quadrant of the New World: salt-preserved splinters of century-old, coolie-laid railroad ties, relics from an earlier era of the Yellow Peril. She burrowed in and began releasing extra clouds of noxious fumes, slipping into epileptic trances, reverting under duress to a seemingly prehistoric style of pure shamaness Shinto, where she daily spread her metaphysical thighs and allowed herself to be possessed by a succession of garrulous demons.

"I'm intrigued," said a honeyed voice from over her younger son's shoulder one searing afternoon. "Everything is so delightfully immanent with your little mommy-san!"

And that was the first time Fukuoka noticed the tall, blue and golden missionary-not one of the Pope's hirelings, but an official emissary in his own right, from another denomination, an all-American one, headquartered in Utah's capital city in the remote, cool, mountainous north.

Young as he was, this missionary called himself "Elder," in place of a first name.

Fukuoka hastened to interpret Mother's babble for the beautiful Elder, to demonstrate that there was absolutely no reason to be intrigued with anything, prayer or scent, that might waft out from under her scrawny rectangle of shade. Even in the extremity of her tongue-lolling, eye bugging, saliva-frothing fits, this woman conjured gods capable of nothing more profound than rote recitations of platitudes. Her utterances suspiciously resembled those issuing from the painted lips of Charlie Chan in the camp movie tent on Friday nights. Okaa-san even sobbed a word that her little boy was sneeringly and gigglingly obliged to translate as Number-One-Son.

And then the letters from Number-One-Son started coming from Alcatraz, long letters in uncensorable kanji. Fukuoka's parents tried to hide them-but where could even a piece of paper be concealed in such a featureless landscape? There was no chest of drawers. Not so much as a hollow tree stump was available.

Fukuoka always located and devoured these letters, for the nutriment his soul found in the elegant handwriting. He practiced long hours in the molten sand with a cactus spine, hypnotized by the varied strokes, the only things in the world that could make him feel even remotely Japanese. But he never could approximate a single one of the myriad beauties of his big brother's hand: the almost musical intermingling of form and content, the spontaneous yet meticulously controlled whips of the brush, producing uncanny marks of "flying white" that preserved not only the horrible and wonderful prison experiences (which Fukuoka hardly compre-hended at the time), but also the very act of expression itself-infinitely more important. And everything was concentrated into a single flow of perfect proportion and balance, qualities lost on his sun-squinting parents.

Younger Brother would at times find himself swooning over the smell of these letters. It seemed almost capable of cover-ing up the family shrine's embarrassing miasma. He would reach up and wave the pages under his new friend's long, white nose, to share the complex aroma of black institutional ink on yellow pris-on stationery.

The golden Elder, of course, being a gaijin, could only assume Fukuoka valued the letters for their content; so he coaxed a translation from boyish lips. He seemed to enjoy especially those passages in which Fukuoka's big brother spoke of "blossoming like a little plum bud" under the tutelage of an enormous Negro, a draft dodger who held court in the prison laundry; and the loss of one's rectal virginity being not quite so wrenching as one might have anticipated throughout one's conscious life.

"Black on yellow, indeed," smiled the Elder. And he would gaze patronizingly on those products of a less vigorous civi-lization: wasting away Father and amulet-fidgeting Mother. It was no problem prying their remaining son away from them.

And, as an eleventh birthday present, along with a forty-minute adventure in the wilderness like nothing the previously sheltered little Fukuoka had ever experienced, the Elder rechristened him.

People of the Elder's faith were not allowed to utter the first syllable of Fukuoka's surname. Indeed, they could hardly bring themselves to think it. Since they traditionally euphemized it flip, that became the child's new name.

And, from that instant of naming, itself the most fundamental form of possessing, the Elder took it upon himself to pray over and lay hands upon his little Flip, to make and destroy and remake his little Flip's entire mind and soul, to conceive and set into motion most of his little Flip's behavior over the following half century.

* * * *

In the desert concentration camp, individuals and families could, with bribes, obtain furloughs. They were permitted to help the local dry farmers scratch up various meager, juiceless and puckered harvests, in return for a by-the-bushel wage that would amuse a Mississippi field slave.

But his older brother was a thief and a political agitator, a federally imprisoned undesirable; so, according to a strict reading of the law of guilt-by-association, little Flip was considered a poor candidate for such luxuriant freedoms. Far from getting a work release to go coax sugar beets from the irrigated foothills of Mount Topaz in the company of his more or less happy coevals, little Flip was allowed only forty minutes on the other side of the barb wire, on one occasion, when the young Elder had wangled him permission to wander in the wilderness.

The Elder more or less commanded him to go out in search of spiritual ecstasies and insights regarding monotheism versus his ancestral animism. There being no need to starve the boy first, the Elder just pried open a padlock with his mighty fingers and discreetly followed his little Flip out into the great desert of the southwestern United States of America.

Hand in hand they explored, briefly, a world of monolithic stone reefs and arches. It was the same as the deserted Iraqi landscape surrounding Ur of the Chaldees, where Abraham's whole life, and the life of humanity, was wrenched inside out by the one and only son-devouring Yahweh. All the sumptuous variety of little Flip's native California was here desiccated into the stern, unyielding Absolute, the dazzling gemstone of truth that outshone his Yamato parents' moral relativism, and their moist, nectar reeking, fur-bearing pantheon.

All the while the golden Elder preached directly into little Flip's ear about one God, an individualistic Father, a single-minded, single-bodied, unbent anthropomorphic thrusting sand-Jehovah, with a purple-turbanned head, and a hardened torso, hairless as a gila monster, standing manly, erect in posture, upon the roughly twin orbs of the Doctrine and the Covenants.

"Forget beets, Sugar," the young Elder had uncharacteristically quipped up close from behind, once the spirit had descended upon little Flip. "You're cut out for a different kind of stoop labor."

In the momentary irreverence of his passion, the Elder's silver voice had aged prematurely; and, for one cloven sub-instant, little Flip, in the deep insecurity of his incarcerated prepubescence, wondered if there was something funny in all this, if the Elder considered it a joke, if he was just another profane Caucasian when the act of emission scratched his proselytizing veneer.

Separating his lids after the first grimace, Flip saw no eyed wheels, no flaming chariots or burning bushes-no bushes of any description-but seemed to have eyes only for the palisades of troops that hooted and cheered on the featureless horizon, and fought over a pair of government issue binoculars to view the scrawny rice-rat's deflowering.

Wobbling in the salted heat waves, they seemed much closer than they really were: whole detachments of guards, white soldiers, melanomizing nicely in the sun, gangling Caucasoid pimple-faces feeling unmasculine because they'd been deemed unworthy to join the struggle overseas, ready at the slightest encouragement to engage in fisticuffs, their thigh-thick arms describing arcs so broad and slow that, to any Japanese, even a nisei like Flip, it seemed anybody with a penknife and the inclination could move in, transplant both gaijin kidneys and return in time for the elephantine fist to obliterate his whole head, and blast a hole deep inside of him.

Flip was a minor, and his parents were aliens, native Japs who couldn't leave the confines of the relocation center; so the Elder tried to lure him away with an offer of a nice orphanage in the green Wasatch foothills up north. "Cool white sheets and pillowcases, sans grit," he snickered. But, in an unacknowledged burst of filial piety, Flip elected to stay with his natural father and mother until his thirteenth birthday.

By that time they had been aged, like lean bacon, with repeated external applications of the salt that traditionally destroyed their compatriots from the inside out. Parched as Palestinians, they were terrified now of the very society they once had seen as a comfy Utopia. Following the vaporization of downtown Hiroshima, Okaa-san and Otoo-san actually had to be forced to leave the concentration camp, expelled from Hell just as from Eden only three years before.

On August thirty-first, 1945, they finally abandoned their younger son in disgust at his new gaijin friends, religion and airs. This was no facile feat; for, in doing so, they rendered themselves spawnless-a bottomless and irrevocable perdition for a couple of familistic Confucians of the old school.

Big Brother, feeling their anguish through long-distance telepathy, tried to re-enter their good graces by renouncing the citizenship he enjoyed by virtue of being born on American soil. But the federal court declared the renunciation void, as made under duress. They would have had to let him out of Alcatraz to repatriate, and they weren't about to let a proved subversive get next to the Soviet Union that easily.

So Mama and Papa cut their losses, pocketed their governmental compensation of ten cents to the dollar, and took advantage of the free ride under Army auspices to Douglas MacArthur's little kingdom in the Pacific, where they promptly and deservingly died, in rapid succession, of blowfish poisoning or stomach cancer or something agonizing and slow and smelly and demeaning like that.

The Elder, convinced of their little boy's visionary

prowess ("a shapely prepubescent Christ to confound the elders," is what he dubbed him), used his connections, of which he had many even then, to declare Flip an orphan after all, and to concoct a dead mother complete with proxy baptism in the Mormon Temple and forged genealogical hard copy. The theology had to be orthodox even if the whole transaction violated every immigration law on the books.

No local family court judge would dare challenge such impeccable credentials. So, after being legally adopted by the Elder and a documented spirit-mother, Flip became the mascot and house boy of one of the more unconventional mission homes to be found along the Wasatch foothills. His baptism by full immersion in a side-freshet of Little Cottonwood Creek was an afternoon to be remembered.

The Opiates of the Mass

Sam and Polly were the first foreigners to have learned Fuzhou City dialect since the communists kicked the missionaries out. Two years of homilies and Gregorian chant transliterated from the Vulgate into the local street lingo had given them a fair proficiency.

Sam had surrounded himself with native speakers who sometimes followed him around, agonized with curiosity. The most curious one yet was tagging along this morning to help celebrate Easter, and now Polly seemed to be sorry they'd ever picked up the language in the first place.

"This is the underground church, not the Patriotic," she whispered. "They take a big enough chance letting me in every week, much less receiving a bicycle full of the likes of you and your friend here. Why do you suppose the congregation needs a fish store as its front? A little discretion, Sammy."

In the courtyard behind the storefront ecclesia, as the tiny removable placard quietly labeled this secret place, the ancient sacristan was squatting in the shade of a banana tree clipping wicks. He was too polite to gawk at the peculiar trio.

"Take a look at this old janitor guy," said Sam, who was in an obnoxious and godless mood today. "Does this old janitor guy look scared? Of course not. These people've got some guts, dear. They're your heroic non-schismatics. They've managed to keep their chins up, even though your Pope betrayed them by upholding the legitimacy of their rivals' apostolic succession. What was the point of these gallant people's depriving themselves of the epidermis and hemoglobin of Jesus Christ all these decades if John-Paul-

John-Paul was going to anoint his infallible crozier with holy oil and f-"

Sam stopped himself short, thinking better of saying the next word in a churchyard. Instead, he took a deep breath and said, "-if he was going to perform the abomination of the Gibeah Benjaminites on them?"

Sam exhaled and bent double to fit through the doorway. To the curious little native who tugged shyly at the tails of his outsized Mao jacket, he murmured, "You're supposed to moisten your pulse-points ever so slightly. This is valid-but-illicit holy water that exists, but isn't supposed to be wet, except it is, anyway."

"That's not holy water," said Polly. "It's baptismal water. And you're not supposed to put your fingers in the font."

"Font my ass," he grunted in street dialect to his sleepy-looking guest. "It's a carp tank in disguise."

Polly also switched to dialect, without meaning to. "If you were going to do this, we should have come last night. There were several infant christenings and we could have fit in less conspicuously." In English, so as not to be rude, she added, "These aren't generic protestants, Sammy. They don't baptize promiscuously in ponds. Adults like her have to go through a period of instruction, and—"

"Oh, her?" Sammy remained in dialect, as rudeness was not a consideration for him. "My little side-kick here? She's already a made-member. Didn't I tell you? Yeah, she already got washed in the Blood of the Lamb, as an infant. Today she's just trying to do her Easter duty. It's the first time since the Great Leap Forward that she's had the courage to come here. She's latched onto me for moral support."

"I've latched onto you," came the tiny voice from behind the billows of his dungarees, "because the party spies will be too busy staring at your red hair and blue eyes to notice me."

"Because of this chick's profession," Sam said, winking, "she's theoretically on the skids with the provincial authorities. But these parishioners are obligated to embrace such a sincere Magdalen, as I keep reminding her. So there's no reason to be scared." He suddenly shifted to a pietistical tone of voice. "See? What did I tell you? Good Father beckons us, all three, to be seated. Let us not keep him waiting. Cover thy head, Jezebel. Let us enter into the One, Holy, Catholic and Apostolic Zorsch."

Whenever he was being sarcastic, just to make sure nobody missed it, he always mispronounced that last word.

The priest, though not thrilled, took this in stride. Sam knew him well and had heard his stories many times. Father had acquired the gift of composure during his thirty-seven years as a prisoner at Qinghai death camp, way out west. He'd administered extreme unction to mad, starving political prisoners, and used his own scant saliva to wash away the original sin of disemboweled, spasming tykes on forced labor teams in the Gobi Desert, and-

The little prostitute's voice started to interrupt, rising up softly from around Sam's knees.

"-was repeatedly beaten senseless with the severed arm of his own altar boy, and forced to have relations with nuns' decapitated corpses, and-"

"Piety brings out the demon in girls like her," whispered Sam. "It'll be all right as long as nobody accidentally rubs an elbow or knee against her."

"Sammy, I'm not sure this is such a good idea," said Polly.

But he had the perfect opportunity to pretend he hadn't heard her; for all the people in the church had paused in their undertakings and cocked their ears in the direction of the fish-emblazoned storefront. Sirens could be heard, a sound that never frightened these people to the point of stopping their singing and praying altogether; but it did give them brief pause whenever it echoed into their secret place of worship.

Nobody was especially nervous: not the silent acolyte who floated among the plastic flowers and Christmas tree lights, his face more like a medieval saint's than any Sam had seen on a living body; not the ancient lady with translucent skin, four-inch feet, and the golden eyes that still condescended even thirty-eight years after her social-climbing warlord husband was smashed by the Reds, and she was liberated and pensioned as a crippled victim of feudalism; and not even the blackened peasant women who pedaled incredible distances every week to be here.

Unfazed by the distant shrieks of storm troopers in full charge, they had all nevertheless jumped out of their skins the first few times Sam had made an entrance. He had to admit that he bore an uncanny resemblance to the large red-bearded Savior that was scrawled on the rectangle of shelf paper and unrolled above the card-table altar each week, the icon of the Redeemer due back any day now for true Liberation, once and for all.

The parishioners' gasps had brought him back to church a few Sundays, at least. He'd squeezed in and out, every time splintering a couple of the child-sized makeshift pews that were disguised during the week as trestle-supports for fish baskets. Weekly replacements were somehow scrounged in this lumber-poor nation, until the heart-breaking novelty of being mistaken for the Parousia wore thin (a pleasure unavailable in the rival Patriotic Church which had canceled the Second Coming in a display of political canniness), and Sam quit attending mass altogether, except for special occasions like today, when he had a street person in tow, needing to re-establish ties with the Divine.

Sam listened to Polly's pals in the tiny congregation wail their caterwauling version of the Kyrie Eleison, set to a microtonal erhu melody from deepest dynastic times. They belted it out with more sheer decibels than he'd ever heard from a first-world parish ten times superior in number and bulk, with ten thousand times the reason to praise God.

Polly approached the lectern to present today's vernacular reading of the Epistle. In her absence Sam's guest finally felt free to speak her mind. This particular class of Chi-com was often diffident in the presence of quality; but that restraint was lifted with only Sam near. Unfortunately, the service was underway and conversation was supposed to have stopped.

"So," she said, "is Heaven an eternity of feeling like you do just before an orgasm, or during an orgasm, or right after an orgasm?"

"How should I know?" said Sam. "Do I look dead yet? I don't even believe in this horse shit."

"Well, I do," she said, "and I'm just thinking about all the different categories of pleasure which God would most likely choose from."

"Yes, well, I have a feeling it wouldn't be quite so pelvic," said Sam.

"Of course, I know that." She took a deep draw on her black pewter canister pipe. "I mean," she exhaled, "it would probably be all in your head, since your body is down here decomposing, right? But I was thinking in terms of intensity. Like, when you're actually in the middle of a climax, I don't think you could maintain that kind of, um, attitude for a very long time. And the before-orgasm kind of pleasure is too suspenseful. After a while you'd get nervous. Afterglow wouldn't be hard to maintain forever, but I'm not sure it wouldn't get boring and sleepy in a few centuries."

"Look," said Sam. "We're not even supposed to be talking now. This is the Consecration and people are trying to be spiritual and you have to shut up. Why don't you ask my wife these questions?"

"Because she's crouching with those people up front."

"That's not exactly crouching. Don't you remember any of this stuff?"

She shrugged her pointy shoulders. Jangling bells called her attention to the elevated host.

"Do you think it's a taste-bud kind of pleasure in Heaven?" She glanced over at Sam's noodle-fed belly. "Maybe it's the pleasure of being nourished. Or maybe there's a kind of pleasure in Heaven that's too elevated for mere scum like me to imagine. Like all the accumulated pleasure I ever felt in my life wouldn't be enough to tickle a single nose hair on God."

"Do you want to get thrown out of here before you've had a chance to fulfill your Paschal obligation? Just keep talking."

That shut her up, for five seconds anyway.

"The Hell part's no problem to imagine," she said, peering out the window and restuffing her tiny pipe bowl with poppy tar. Then she sneered at the pale lady with the bound feet seated a few trestles up. "That one already had her turn in Heaven. I wonder if God's idea of pleasure is wadding the feet up like pieces of toilet paper."

She presented to Sam her own blackened, splayed feet. "And they say there are no streetwalkers in the People's Republic. I may have stayed away from here till now, but I can kneel a lot longer than any of these holy folks-and on cobblestones, too, not just this cushy asphalt tile."

Sam decided to take the pipe away, again. Maybe a few breaths of unadulterated South China soot would instill a little quietude. After a brief and indecisive wrestle among the mimeographed hymnals, he tried to reason with her.

"See that man depicted on the shelf paper? You should abstain in honor of the day he finished harrowing Hell. He folded his linen neatly, rolled back the rock, and walked around unrecognizable to his best friends, convincing them of his legitimacy by displaying these five holes in his body.

She was unimpressed. "A couple extra holes, so what?"

"Yeah, but nail holes. Like jumbo God-sized tracks."

But she didn't buy that either. A slate-grey haze was gathering in the house of God, and the regulars were coughing and glancing over their shoulders. That stinking pacifier of hers had to go out the window. It would be a shame if she had to be defenestrated along with it, when she'd only just entered the fold that week.

One thing was certain: if she was hell-bent on making communion, she'd have to shuffle up the aisle under her own steam, for Sam's whole hefty metabolism recoiled like an albino vampire from the Real Presence. That was why he always sat in the back.

His mom was low-church Episcopalian, and at her liberal knee he'd learned the very definition of the word "symbolism" by coolly contemplating the poetical nicety of the wine and bread. This morning his otherwise rational wife was trembling before a wafer-thin slice of the sole material that put her in divergence with post-seventeenth-century thought. It would be terrifying to approach something that substantial with a head full of attitudes flip as Sam's. He was sure he'd see wads of gristle and scab.

But the little flat-backer hankered after it, and nothing in her background cheapened it dangerously. As the pipe bounced off the window sill and clanked among the wild poinsettias, grey tears of sweat began to flop out from under her double eyelids. Soon she'd be in no shape to sit up straight, much less balance on her knees at the splintery plywood rail, eyes closed, mouth open. She needed something smokeless to fortify her, at least until the Canon was over and her long march to the communion rail could begin.

Then a solution occurred to him-about twelve percent, as a matter of fact.

Sam's doctor had given him a few handfuls of Hungarian blue morphine ampules, in case he got a kidney stone attack out of crawling range of the provincial hospital. Just an occasional half-squirt or so was all he was allowed to self-administer, subcutaneously, and not as a euphoric, but just enough to serve as a muscle relaxant in case a few uric acid crystals got wedged against any especially sensitive bundles of nerve endings.

Not wanting to be the one to introduce yet another vice into her squalid life, he fiddled with the tiny bottles in his lap a long time, making sure the little prostitute got a good look, to see if she'd recognize them, which she did.

"That's smoke you put in your arm," she said admiringly, and began to mourn the absence of an "arm pipe," as the contrivance was termed in her vernacular.

Ah, Chinese, the language of imagism.

He hoped things wouldn't get too sordid, that it wouldn't be necessary to show her how to use the disposable syringes which he'd liberated from the forced AIDS tests for non-Russian foreigners at the municipal gymnasium-and it wasn't necessary. Sam only had to show her how to unwrap everything, and had to demonstrate just once, to prove that these light-weight plastic toys were as effective as the two-pound cast iron spikes she stole from the rag pickers who scavenged out behind the Sanitation Workers' Clinic and rinsed with stringy mucus from the open sewers.

She'd never seen a throw-away needle; as a member of the Flower and Willow Lane work unit, she'd never seen anything disposable but females and prophylactics. But she burrowed under his overhanging gut and removed Sam's belt almost before he could offer it as a tourniquet, and began to take steps toward mollifying herself into a reasonable pew-mate.

This was a fane, a place for inculcating comfy faith; and she looked as though she could use a bedtime story to cling to, an indulgence, before she inevitably nodded off. She plainly had no plans to pay attention to the professional homilist exercising his lungs at the podium now. So Sam decided to step in and murmur to her about the most obvious person to be murmured about in a situation like this.

Instead of poking around for uncollapsed blood vessels with brain-dead junkie tarts, Polly was worshipping three rows up alongside the only clear thinkers in the People's Republic of China: men and women, mostly women, who had the sense to recognize their own history as a perfect illustration of the futility of throwing oneself into the arms of a secular, therefore fallible, savior.

So Sam took his cue from them. He started softly preaching about the creator of the first and only paradise in the history of the oldest, biggest civilization, which is the closest thing to the miraculous ever accomplished by a mortal. After Liberation, this certain person gave one out of every four people on earth a sojourn in Eden, the Seven Good Years. The city parks were admission-free, nobody ever shoved on queues, and the party's materialistic idealism served as a fresh moral force among the youth. Millions of flesh-and-blood Lei Fengs strode around in their cloth shoes doing good things as, for the first time in history, a commie economy was on the rise. Western observers were wetting their pants.

But even Nero had his quinquennium. The Great Helmsman slouched duly into his dotage and frightened off poor Khrushchev with his enthusiasm to nuke America. This left the economy on its own to deal with his senile megalomaniacal dream of overnight industrialization. Mao destroyed paradise just as surely as he'd created it: serpent and God the Father rolled into one chubby little carcass.

"My wife's trestle-mates," Sam was saying, "most of them peasants and lumpen-types like you, have shown the intuitive sense to put their faith in someone who actually claimed to be God, no pussy-footing, no false modesty about it, who offered them literal perfection, manifest to their eyes at least eventually, who promised that he wouldn't die and go away and leave them in the slimy, bloody hands of a Lu Shaoqi or a Lin Biao, but in the stone-cold hands of-hey, wait a minute! Don't forget to get the air bubbles out of the line before you shoot that stuff up."

She ignored him, rolled up her gaudy sleeve and displayed her stigmata as proof of something Sam had never doubted. "I thought we weren't supposed to talk," she said.

"We're not. My wife's pew-mates believe in someone who didn't require a mausoleum to contain the tissues he left behind, his head lit up bright yellow from within like a latex jack- o'- lantern, but who, on the contrary, even made special, more or less unprecedented arrangements for his body to vanish and go some- place far, far away, so that no matter how bad his executors and successors and administrators fucked up, no matter how many mil- lions of people got burned, tortured, maimed and killed in faction- al power struggles and other forms of holy and just warfare, you always had the sneaking suspicion that he might return and fix things up and kick you in the butt. Here, flip the reservoir like this, see? That's why it's made of transparent plastic—so you can see the bubbles. Just relax! I'll give it back to you!

"The Helmsman/Savior whom my wife's pew-mates buy into cleverly harnesses the power of your own imagination with his claims to perfection, and you do most of the work for him. He's as nearly perfect as your dreamy, faithful brain can make him out to be. And the sky's the limit, because there's no visible competi- tion. You can do the In-Tourist shtick and schlep yourself over to Moscow on the train and see the embalming job they did on Lenin; you can go down to the People's Republic of Vietnam and check out the seams around Ho Chih Minh's hairline: but where can you go to find a rival for somebody who was shrewd enough to fix it so he can't be seen except in your head?

"The guy had class," continued Sam, again directing her gaze up at the picture behind the card table altar. "He never said a single overtly political thing, but just sniffed off the whole ques- tion with his 'render unto Caesar' line. Yet he carried out a pro- found coup on the imagination, as indicated by the presence of Polly's pals and the priest and the acolyte, all bearing the lumps, bumps and extra holes of past purges.

"No, I'm not being an old woman. Do you want to get bubbles in your head and die like a sap? And this junk's pharma- ceutical. You don't need to filter it, for Christ's sake! Is this the first time you ever heard the good news?"

Tom Bradley

She naturally thought he was referring to the good news of pre-filtered Hungarian blue morphine in convenient snap-top ampules.

"Of course not," she said, momentarily forgetting the needle in her indignation at being accused of ignorance in such essential matters. She was expert enough in the opiates of the mass. "But we see arm-smoke and arm-pipes only on special occasions at my dan wei," she said, "Like when major cadres roll through Flower and Willow Lane with slumming on their minds. They call it 'linking with the masses.' High-tone girls up in Qingdao and Dalian smell nicer, and their skin is smoother and whiter, but they don't push back and don't like to get even the tiniest bit rough."

"Yeah?" said Sam. He stared down a couple of indignant parishioners. "Sounds to me like they've been trained in the phony imitation-geisha style."

"That's exactly right," she marveled, gazing at him with almost as much admiration as she had at the ampules. "You bignoses really know your vice and corruption, don't you?"

When she looked back down at her forearm, she couldn't believe the point had entered, so accustomed she was to the blunt repeaters of the street. The one-time-only shaft seemed to rattle from side to side, to click against the edges of the permanently enlarged skin pore that she'd excavated as a conduit to blow the blue smoke into the crotch of her elbow.

Before consummating this union, she tantalized herself with a few seconds' delay. She held her thumb cocked like a pistol hammer over the syringe and looked up at the ceiling in anticipation.

She said, "Those imperialist Japanese swine disemboweled my mother and father in Stalin Square. They caused me to wind up like I am, like most pretty orphan girls. And now their weakling style of partying procures me influential customers. Chubby neo-Dengist bureaucrats, most of them."

She slammed the plunger home, then pumped it a few times to rinse the line with some of her own blood. Her eyes suddenly went dim over junk-sucked cheeks, and her body started to seep between the splinters of the trestle. She seemed pretty intent on taking a nap against Sam's right love-handle, apparently assuming the giant American would stick around and nudge her when the time came.

"Not so much," he said, fighting the urge to slide out and leave her to bonk her head on the pew. He punched her gently but firmly. "You have to be awake to take the Eucharist. It's almost your turn."

She tugged at his sleeve and moaned, "You may not know it, big brother, but Jesus is in your head. And you're trying to put him in mine. That's where he'll eventually have to be if I'm going up to Heaven without my body. But in the meantime, I want him inside me, here."

She rubbed her belly and lower abdomen. She looked sadly toward the front of the fish store, then down at her rubbery legs.

Father reached out his hand and beckoned this small soul toward home. She started to nod off. The priest sighed and made moves toward replacing the remaining hosts in his pyx.

Sam decided to swallow his horror and approach the macabre card table with its goblet full of gore. He grabbed a knobby little elbow and proceeded slowly up the aisle, his other hand around her shoulder.

"Here we go, little sister," he whispered.

The Life and Times of LaFontaine the Mesmerizer

The pointed finger of the stage hypnotist was the same
finger used by ancient healers in the Temple of Sleep.
—John-Ivan Palmer

It's 1874, and he is having one of his usual triumphs. Huge and perfect, a demigod with a mountain of shining black curls on his head, he stands on the stage of the freshly built Paris Opera House.

The place is a neo-baroque marvel, with marble statues, jewel-studded arches, crystal chandeliers and gold-leafed pillars gleaming everywhere. The vast dome overhead features a fresco of God in his Heaven, being serenaded by hundreds of plump, rosy angels.

Several princes are in the audience, along with marquises, duchesses and various other continental glitterati of the time, each dressed more beautifully than the next. It's a capacity crowd, and they're all on their feet, loudly expressing their amazement, and their love, for Monsieur LaFontaine, the greatest of all mesmerizers.

He bows gracefully as red roses rain down on him. He waves massive, white-gloved hands through the air like a magician or a priest.

Stretched out before him is a young noblewoman, completely under his power. She looks like an angel in a white satin gown. Her body is suspended between two intricately carved rosewood chairs which touch only the back of her neck and her ankles.

"You hear only my voice," LaFontaine tells her, and what she hears is magnificent. "Your will is not your own, but has merged with the vital fluid that emanates from my mind..."

* * * *

He stands majestically in the middle of the floor in an opulent Parisian parlor, furnished in the most elaborate style of the day.

It's a soirée of late 19th-century Europe's most brilliant intelligentsia, including a poet, a few artists, a couple of philosophers and their aristocratic hangers-on. The host is a fabulously wealthy nouveau riche from the world of international finance, who knows just enough to keep his mouth shut. Also present, of course, are several of the world's most beautiful women. They stare at LaFontaine, enrapt, flushed with spiritual aspirations.

Remaining aloof is Baron Dupotet. Plump and swarthy, with a cruelly sensual mouth and serpent's eyes, he simmers with envy.

"Monsieur LaFontaine!" says one of the philosophers. "I heard you were languishing in a southern prison."

"And so I was. The king of Naples allowed me to roll the stone from the sepulcher and come forth."

A painter says, "Surely you mesmerized his Neapolitan majesty to gain such clemency."

"He did set one condition," says LaFontaine.

"Which was?"

"That I cease restoring sight to the blind and hearing to the deaf."

"But, Monsieur LaFontaine," says the poet, "why would the king have you behave so uncharitably toward the wretches of this world?"

"A small matter of the all-too-faithful imitation of Christ."

Everyone titters at this near-blasphemous remark, except Baron Dupotet.

"You imitate Christ, LaFontaine?" he bellows. "Bah! Mesmerism's pretensions toward healing were pooh-poohed a hundred years ago by no less a personage than Doctor Guillo-tine—"

"—who deserved to be consulted on the topic of staying healthy," says a beautiful woman. "Right up till the moment of death."

More titters are heard.

LaFontaine looks at her with chaste appreciation, and she nearly melts under his eyes. He turns to deal with the baron.

"It's a matter, my dear Dupotet, of psychologizing—or 'animal-magnetizing', as you would inaccurately say—the astral body, which is poised intermediate between the spiritual and phys-ical—"

"I don't require schooling on the rudiments of our art."

"But I'm afraid you do. I wouldn't call it 'our' art, in any case."

Baron Dupotet swells with anger.

The poet looks as though he'll expire like a delicate flower if this conflict escalates any further. He withdraws from the inner circle and approaches a purple couch situated in the corner among exotic potted ferns.

Sitting upon this couch is a seven-foot-tall Punjabi Hindu. Curled up next to him is a Roman Catholic cardinal, capped and robed in red satin, an envoy from the Vatican. He's almost as tall as the Hindu, and is obviously his lover—for tonight, at any rate.

The Hindu wears a vast white turban with a fist-sized ruby pinned at the helm. Wrapped in the serpentine hose of an exquisite jade hookah, he shares slow sips of soup-thick narcotic smoke with the Cardinal. The two of them listen to LaFontaine with a pleased look in their eyes.

The poet tries to appropriate some opiated hashish from an alabaster box which the Hindu holds in the palm of one gigantic hand.

"That's soma," says the Hindu. "Or something near enough. It's not intended for profane consumption. Aryans only."

"But," replies the poet, "those two megalomaniacs are going to draw stilettos any moment. It's so unpleasant to have corpses bleeding underfoot at soirées this time of year."

"I'm enjoying their contretemps," yawns the Cardinal.

"LaFontaine is quite good."

"But the Baron needs mollification," says the poet.

The poet and the Hindu have a friendly mock battle over the narcotic morsel, slapping one another's hands away. The poet prevails, and comes away in triumph with the prize.

The cardinal calls after him, "Don't mollify our two wonder-workers too much. His Eminence, the Holy Father in Rome, has a very important job for both of them."

The poet lays the hashish on the green marble mantelpiece and proceeds to knead it together with some potent-looking herbs from his waistcoat pocket. The resulting concoction is nestled in golden spoons and passed around on a silver tray.

Baron Dupotet gobbles two helpings, then three. His eyes grow red and aggressive with intoxication.

"So, LaFontaine," he leers, "do you have your way with those lovely young subjects of yours?"

Glancing at Dupotet's plump belly, LaFontaine replies, "I'm not quite so comfortably confined in my coat of flesh as you are in yours, Monsieur le Baron."

Dupotet is enraged by that remark. He snatches a golden spoon of the hashish mixture and brandishes it in LaFontaine's face like a poisoned dagger.

The great mesmerist turns aside in revulsion.

"Unlike yours, Dupotet, my body plays host to no demons that demand nourishment."

* * * *

At the bottom of a hole in a Victorian London graveyard lies a woman. She's dead, as it happens, but is being rousted from her eternal repose by a couple of Cockney resurrectionists, whose illegal vocation is to supply the medical community with bodies to dissect.

"Right, Jasper. Be so pleasant as to grab that trotter. Heave-ho."

A dark, plump figure hovers in the shadows behind a nearby gravestone, supervising these two louts—though they are unaware of his existence. Baron Dupotet has not bothered to introduce himself to his subjects.

"Gin and pies tonight, as they say at Buckingham Palace." The two resurrectionists carry the dead woman through the darkness, discreetly stuffed in a burlap bag. They approach the back door of the Royal College of Surgeons, giving wide berth to a paid-off bobbie who stands in their path, very obviously paying no attention.

A white-coated surgeon admits the resurrectionists with their load, whispering, "Make haste, make haste, you two... er, three."

An entity slides out of the shadows and slips unnoticed into the college on the resurrectionists' heels. Before the door can close, he glances back over his shoulder, revealing himself to be Baron Dupotet.

* * * *

In no time the cadaver's delivered to a dissection room, and a professor goes to work, soberly and respectfully. His interns gather around, paying clinical attention. Few of them ogle her bosom, and none sees Monsieur le Baron creep past the door.

He moves down a corridor softly gas-lit and quiet as a temple, past a series of chambers where macabre but useful studies are being pursued.

Baron Dupotet sneaks into a lecture hall, unseen, and leans against the back wall. He has come to heckle his rival, LaFontaine, who stands at the podium, delivering a formal lecture.

The great mesmerizer has dressed himself a bit more soberly for this occasion than he does for his public performances and soirees. His manner and voice are modulated for the academic circumstances. But he is no less impressive for that.

The lecture hall is full of frowzy old physicians of various specialties. In their outdated frock coats, wire-rim spectacles and bushy gray beards down to their watch-chains, these codgers look as though they wouldn't crack a smile if LaFontaine were to levitate the whole building, or cause elves to materialize.

They listen to him carefully, anyway. It's clear, from the sceptical look in their eyes and the sardonic way they stroke their whiskers, that they want only to dissect his ideas and expose them as unscientific. But LaFontaine seems to be getting through to a number of their younger colleagues, who stand at the back, unaware of the baron's presence among them.

"Gentlemen," LaFontaine is saying, "please be aware that mesmerism entails the conscious or, indeed, unconscious projection of the vital fluid. Certain deluded amateurs insist on describing this process as 'animal-magnetism.'"

He glances at Dupotet, who swells with anger, and screams, "We'll see who's deluded!"

Nobody but LaFontaine heard that.

As if nothing has happened, LaFontaine continues his lecture. "The potency of the vital fluid is determined by the mesmerist's spiritual status and moral condition. Herein lies the danger of the practice. For if the mesmerist is corrupt of heart, foul of mind, and diseased of soul..."

Dupotet bows, as if acknowledging a compliment and accepting applause.

"...the vital fluid which he projects will be tainted. Under such influence, the subject can become morally and spiritually weakened. And this will constitute a grave danger to the subject's life."

LaFontaine is mildly distressed to see the baron vanish.

* * * *

Seven huge, blond, blue-eyed Swiss guards, in elaborate ceremonial armor and helmets, shouldering lethal-looking halberds, march down a splendiferous hallway.

The ceilings are gold-leafed, and burnished bronze statues stand in niches every few yards. The walls are covered with frescoes of magnificent saints, as befits the Vatican's papal residence in the Year of Our Lord, 1882.

At the end of this fabulous hallway is a pair of cast-bronze doors which depict grandiose and grotesque scenes from Dante. Two more colossal Swiss guards stand sentry to the left and right.

An old man, short and stooped, hobbles along in the Swiss guards' midst. Wearing a full-length white satin robe and skull-cap, it's none other than His Eminence, Pope Pius IX. His Grace is an obese old lecher, with puffy lips and swollen lower eyelids, heavily made up. There's an expression perpetually fixed on his face which makes him look as though he just had an orgasm or two.

Pope Pius IX arrives at the big bronze doors, and the guards swing them open to reveal the private papal audience chamber, a mighty room straight from the glory days of Michelangelo. It's full of marble statuary and boasts a coffered mahogany ceiling with a vast chandelier. On an alabaster table is a selection of five different kinds of wine in crystal carafes.

Standing at that table is Baron Dupotet. Seeing the pope, he quickly puts down a glass of gravy-thick burgundy that he's been swilling without permission. He begins to cross himself with great fervency.

Standing nearby, mildly amused, is LaFontaine.

A fat, gore-colored ruby weighs down the flounder-pale forefinger of Pope Pius IX. Baron Dupotet falls promptly on his knees and commences fellating it.

Soon it's LaFontaine's turn. Choosing not to kneel, but only to bend slightly at the waist, LaFontaine brings his lips correctly close to the tasteless bauble, but no closer.

The Holy Father says, "Gentlemen, let us wish and hope that, for the good of humanity, animal-magnetism may soon be generally employed for the benefit of..."

"I prefer the term 'mesmerism'," says LaFontaine.

Baron Dupotet, still on his knees, pretends to be shocked at his rival's rudeness. The pope reddens, but chooses to ignore the interruption.

"I encourage you, my sons, to continue your magnificent work, in the confidence that it will enhance the spiritual well-being of all Christendom. The blessings of Our Lord and Savior, Jesus Christ, be with you."

"Amen," says the baron.

Pope Pius IX pauses for LaFontaine to say, "Amen." It going to be quite a wait, if the look on his face is any indication.

His Eminence fondles a sapphire and emerald rosary that would make Marie Antoinette want to use the bidet. He looks into LaFontaine's eyes.

LaFontaine looks back into his—not hypnotically, not even in defiance, but with disdain. The Amen doesn't seem to be forthcoming.

Five delicious altar boys, all golden curls, sapphire eyes and pudgy pink dimples, suck with pouting lips on almonds and grapes. They lounge languidly on purple velvet cushions strewn about the pearl-encrusted taffeta slippers of Pope Pius IX.

The Holy Father seats himself upon a throne that would make Nero feel like the Whore of Babylon. Baron Dupotet and LaFontaine take up positions before him, the former ogling the altar boys, the latter fastidiously averting his gaze.

His Holiness observes LaFontaine's eyes alighting upon one child who sits apart from the rest.

"Can either of you wonder-workers mesmerize a smile onto that gloomy little wretch? As you have probably guessed, he's the reason I summoned you."

The boy, dark and severe, sits up straight, spine locked. He shrinks from contact with the corrupted altar boys, preferring the hard marble floor to a velvet cushion in their scented midst. Perhaps a tad frail, but handsome, even at his tender age he is revolted by the decadence that surrounds him.

"As you can see," says the pope, "he's a Jew from the countryside. Son of a bailiff. A Christian servant girl baptized him in secret, but left him otherwise untouched."

"Wasteful girl," leers Baron Dupotet.

The pope snickers. LaFontaine does not respond.

"The baptism was performed in a papal state, so, according to church law, he must be raised a Catholic. I've taken him under my wing, so to speak."

The altar boys giggle.

"That's a funny thing to call it."

"I've heard you call it many names, Your Holiness, but never a wing."

"Silence! In the knotted bowels of Christ, I adjure you to hold those pink tongues!"

The Holy Father flings a massive, bejeweled, solid-gold chalice at the smart alecks, braining one of them in a splash of purple wine. This strikes the baron as quite funny. He suppresses laughter. His plump belly jiggles, and he holds one hand over his mouth.

The altar boys watch Dupotet's belly, and giggle some more.

This enrages the Supreme Pontiff further. "You little heathens find this humorous? I'll cause my most colossal guard to skewer all of you at once on his halberd! He'll flick you down to Hell like so many flies—though I know Satan will be angry with me for cluttering up his abode with such pallid trash!"

"Oh, Daddy wouldn't do that," says the plumpest altar boy. He eyes the colossal guard in question, who happens to be standing at attention against the nearest wall.

LaFontaine looks up in surprise, and is appalled to see this giant has precisely the same blue eyes, golden hair and ample pale flesh as the altar boys. It's obvious he's fathered at least three of them.

With pouting lips, on hands and knees like an infant, the plumpest altar boy starts sidling up to his daddy.

The colossal guard's sanctified job is to stand like a statue and never move except to shield the pope from assassination or abduction. Now he has broken into a sweat under his nine-pound helmet. He wears an agonized look on his table-sized face, and tries, with frantic eye movements, to tell his creeping brat to shut up and back off.

Caressing Daddy's big boot, the boy murmurs, "You wouldn't be so mean as to poke me with your big pokey thing, would you, Da-a-a-addy?"

He leers at his own reflection in his daddy's standard Vatican-issue shin-bone armor, then slowly gets up on his pudgy little haunches and starts to fondle the poor man's steel knee-spike.

Dupotet can contain himself no longer. Pointing first at the knee-spike, then to the brat who licks and tickles it, he explodes in belly laughs.

"The little... The filthy... Oh, Mother Mary hemorrhaging on a close stool!"

"You are dismissed, Monsieur le Baron," says the pope, icily.

No longer laughing, but quite unhappy, Baron Dupotet is escorted out.

LaFontaine has a brief moment to ponder the little Jewish boy. He is charmed by the lad, in a chaste, fatherly way.

Pope Pius IX says, "Your incontinent colleague—who will remain nameless throughout Christendom till the Day of Reckoning, if I have anything to say about it—once told me that young children are especially easy to, shall we say, put under one's 'animal-magnetic' power. Malleable little souls, and so forth. Can you do anything with this small son of Abraham, Isaac and so forth? I'll make it worth your while, Monsieur LaFontaine."

What little reverence there might have been in LaFontaine's eyes is gone now. With infinite tenderness, and without permission, he gathers up the little Jewish boy from the marble floor.

The latter allows himself to be lifted into LaFontaine's arms. But the stiffness of his posture indicates that it's only because he needs to be rescued, not because he submits to being loved. Not yet, anyway.

LaFontaine turns his back on Pope Pius IX, a grave offense in itself. He could be chopped to bits any moment. Without genuflecting, groveling, or even asking leave, LaFontaine vacates the papal audience chamber, taking the Jewish boy with him.

The colossal guard makes a lunge, as if to cut the mesmerist down in his tracks. But the Holy Father stops him.

"I wouldn't advise you to raise hands against that man."
Stunned by his god-like boss' warning, the colossal guard gasps, "Is he Satan's henchman, Your Eminence?"

"We should be so fucking lucky."

* * * *

LaFontaine exits the Papal apartments, carrying the little Jewish boy. Gently, he deposits the boy in a carriage, says a few words to the driver, and gets in. They rattle off down the sanctified cobble stones of Saint Peter's Square.

* * * *

There's a sea of pale faces at the London Zoological Gardens, including those belonging to Queen Victoria, her Prime Minister Benjamin Disraeli, her pet poet Alfred Lord Tennyson, and assorted other royalist big-wigs of 1884.

They're all seated comfortably in armchairs under a grand silken pavilion which shades them from the halfhearted English sun. Her Majesty seems to be enchanted, perhaps even mesmerized, by something that is taking place before her eyes in the lion's cage.

Inside the cage, whose bars have been gilded for the occasion and spiraled around with ribbons of red and blue silk, stands LaFontaine. At his feet, an enormous lion lies flat on its back, its four mighty legs sticking straight up in the air.

The Jewish boy is in the cage, too, grown a couple well-nourished and -loved years' worth. He looks much more comfortable in the company of a large carnivore than he was in the pope's.

He has been educated, trained, and splendidly dressed in a red velvet Little Lord Fauntleroy outfit. This young son of Abraham, Isaac and Jacob is obviously having the time of his life. He possesses all the stage presence of a professional two or three times his age.

In his grandest manner, LaFontaine says, "The vital fluid fills all space and all beings."

The Jewish boy says, "Gauche!"

On that command, the lion's paws move left, and Queen Victoria murmurs in admiration, as do the members of her entourage.

LaFontaine says, "To control the vital fluid is to control all things, and all beings."

"Droit!" cries the Jewish boy.

The beastly paws move to the right, and Alfred Lord Tennyson begins to applaud, even before his sovereign sets the precedent.

"Will is limitless!" says LaFontaine.

The Jewish boy cries, "Epées mortelles!" causing the lion's huge claws to pop out.

Tom Bradley

Her Majesty gasps, "Jesus Christ! Look at those big sharp cock-suckers!"

The royalist big wigs begin to applaud, thinking the claw display to be LaFontaine's climax. They are unable to imagine anything more spectacular. But then the great mesmerist nods at his little assistant.

"You may do the honors, my esteemed colleague."

When the Jewish boy flicks an index finger in the air, the lion leaps to its feet and claws the red and blue silk ribbons off the gilded bars.

Queen Victoria squawks, soils her regal drawers, and faints.

* * * *

Incognito, caped and hooded, a perfumed handkerchief shielding his nose, LaFontaine disapprovingly observes a poor performance of Baron DuPotet in a Victorian London working-class dive.

The baron's audience is composed of Ripper-bait street-walkers, pickpockets, housebreakers, waterside characters and other sundry wretched members of the Dickensian lumpenproletariat. Unwashed, very pale, everybody's swilling gin, bellowing sea shanties and mostly ignoring Dupotet.

He stands on a stage contrived of broken boat planks laid across empty gin barrels. Looking the worse for wear, clothes rusty and rumpled, face unshaven, the self-styled "animal-magnetizer" seems to have fallen on tough times since pissing off Pope Pius IX.

Dupotet has selected, or coerced, an old whore to be his subject – rather, victim. To the dull amusement of the sodden clientele, he grabs a pepper shaker from a fat Cockney who's gobbling meat pies, and shoves a handful up the old whore's nose. She doesn't react at all. Due to post-hypnotic suggestion, her body remains insensate.

He bows, giving a flourish of the pepper shaker, and gets nothing but a few burps in response. He determines to escalate his assaults on the old whore, because he is starved for applause. Dupotet approaches her with a loaded and cocked pistol in his hand, and fires it right up next to her ear. She flinches not at all.

Dupotet commences stitching the old whore's lips together with carpet thread. She utters no complaint.

Bobbies, tin whistles shrieking, come in and close down Baron Dupotet's show, taking him into custody, respectfully. He is a baron, after all. They permit him a final bow, to which nobody responds.

On the way out, manacled, he tries to engage LaFontaine one last time. "Come for the gin and pies, Monsieur?"

LaFontaine, keeping his perfumed handkerchief to his nose, doesn't even look at Dupotet. To the bobbies, he says, "I am sorry to say that the baron is, loosely speaking, my colleague. I'm obliged to linger here and repair his damage."

LaFontaine waits for them to escort Dupotet away. Then he approaches the makeshift stage. With infinite gentleness, he reaches out a hand toward the old whore's ruined face.

"Your will is not your own," says LaFontaine, "but has merged with the vital fluid that emanates from my mind..."

The old whore has powder burns on the side of her head from the pistol DuPotet discharged next to it; she has blood coming from her nostrils, due to the caustic pepper he forced into them; her lips are a mass of carnage, held together with coarse sutures of carpet thread.

LaFontaine passes his right hand over her three times. On the third pass, his hand stops, covering her poor face.

"Universal forces hold your astral body in suspension, like a pearl dissolved in ocean water... I transmit the vital fluid from my mind to your body."

When LaFontaine withdraws his hand, we see that the old whore's nose has stopped hemorrhaging. Not only the blood and powder burns, but the dirt, scars and pock marks of her previous depraved existence are all smoothed away. She still has plenty of wrinkles, but they're the laugh-lines of someone's sweet old granny having an afternoon nap.

In a gentler, more intimate tone, LaFontaine says, "And, of course, my good woman, you instinctively know the other name for the vital fluid."

Tom Bradley

Dreamily, she shifts her dear head to one shoulder. When she smiles, the carpet thread puffs away like so many filaments of angel hair. Just barely audible, her reply is more of a sigh than a syllable.

* * * *

At the Paris Opera House, the angelic noblewoman in the white satin gown is suspended between the two rosewood chairs.

The great mesmerist is absorbing all the admiration and love of a standing ovation, delivered by the most beautiful human beings on the earth. He takes a final bow.

Thank you very much, ladies and gentlemen.

About the Author

Tom Bradley received his novelist's calling at the age of nineteen. He climbed into the moonlit mountains around his hometown, where he got an unambiguous vocation with physical symptoms and everything, just like Martin Luther in the electric storm. He doesn't recall being on acid at the time. He buzzed permanently off from America in 1985, moved to Red China, and has lurked around the left rim of the Pacific ever since, in a successful search for sinecures that steal virtually no time and absolutely no mental energy from his writing. Further curiosity can be indulged at *tombradley.org*

Also by Tom Bradley

Family Romance (with Nick Patterson)
Bomb Baby
Put It Down in a Book
My Hands Were Clean/Dr. Gonzo (with Deb Hoag)
Calliope's Boy
Even the Dog Won't Touch Me
Hemorrhaging Slave of an Obese Eunuch
Lemur
Vital Fluid
Epigonesia (with Kane X. Faucher)
Fission Among the Fanatics
Hustling the East
The Curved Jewels
Kara-kun, Flip-kun
Black Class Cur
Acting Alone
Killing Bryce

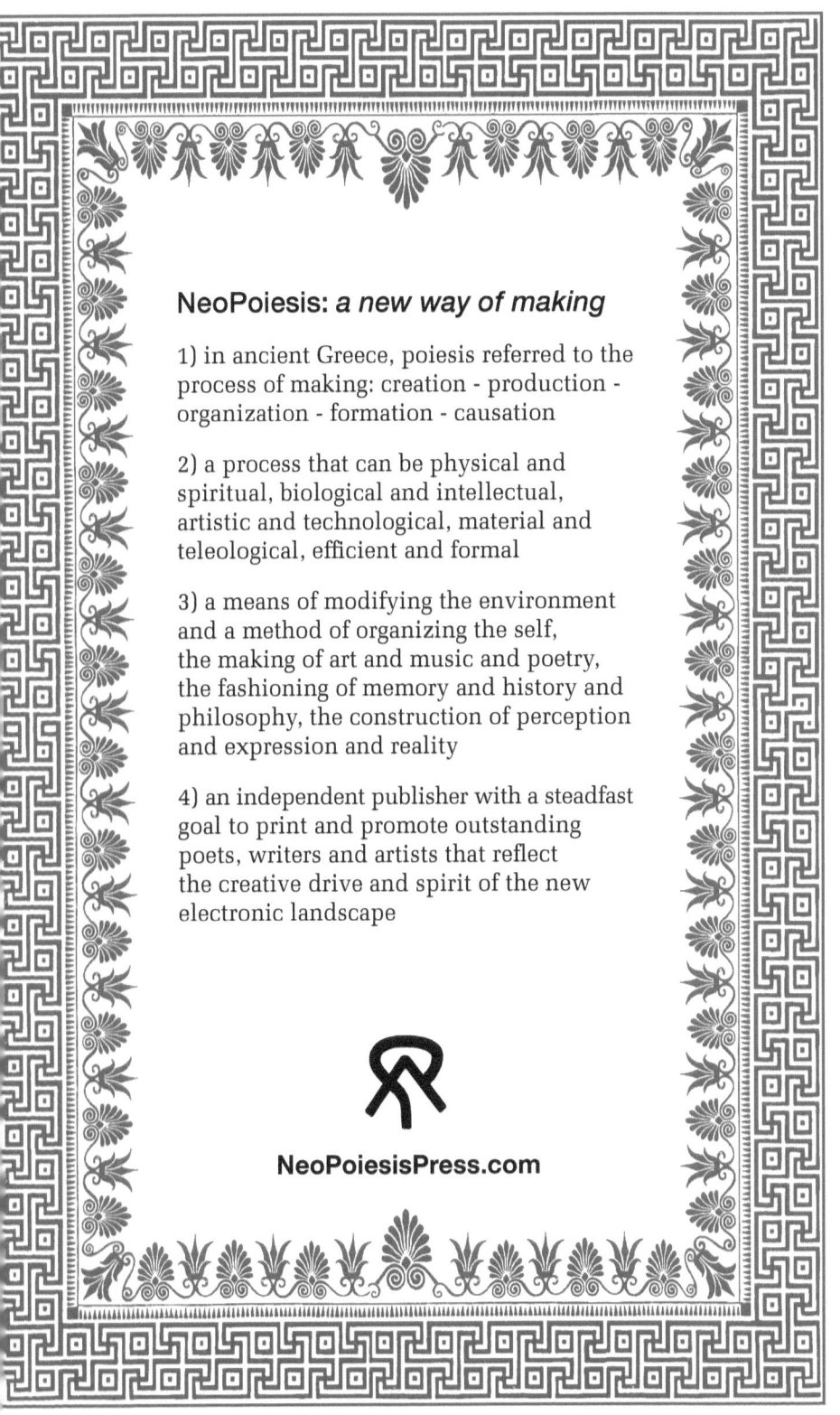

NeoPoiesis: *a new way of making*

1) in ancient Greece, poiesis referred to the process of making: creation - production - organization - formation - causation

2) a process that can be physical and spiritual, biological and intellectual, artistic and technological, material and teleological, efficient and formal

3) a means of modifying the environment and a method of organizing the self, the making of art and music and poetry, the fashioning of memory and history and philosophy, the construction of perception and expression and reality

4) an independent publisher with a steadfast goal to print and promote outstanding poets, writers and artists that reflect the creative drive and spirit of the new electronic landscape

NeoPoiesisPress.com

www.ingramcontent.com/pod-product-compliance
Lightning Source LLC
Chambersburg PA
CBHW020655260626
47157CB00008B/3043